"It's crazy to think that you'd be attracted to me."

"It is?" That green gaze was intense on her face and then it slid down her body.

"Of course it is," she said. "I'm so fat and unattractive..."

"You're pregnant," he said. "And you're beautiful."

She laughed. "I wasn't fishing for compliments. I know exactly what I look like—a whale."

"I would not be attracted to a whale."

"You're not attracted to me." She wished he was. But it wasn't possible. Even if she wasn't pregnant, she knew he would never go for a woman like her.

He stepped closer, his gaze still hot on her face and body. "I'm not?"

She shook her head. But he caught her chin and stopped it. Then he tipped up her chin and lowered his head. And his lips covered hers.

THE PREGNANT WITNESS

LISA CHILDS

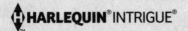

HARLEQUIN® INTRIGUE®

To Kimberly Duffy—with great appreciation for all
our years of friendship! You're the best!

ISBN-13: 978-0-373-69823-3

The Pregnant Witness

Copyright © 2015 by Lisa Childs

PLEASE RECYCLE
THIS PRODUCT IS RECYCLABLE

Recycling programs
for this product may
not exist in your area.

Printed in U.S.A.

www.Harlequin.com

Lisa Childs writes paranormal and contemporary romance for Harlequin. She lives on thirty acres in Michigan with her two daughters, a talkative Siamese, and a long-haired Chihuahua who thinks she's a rottweiler. Lisa loves hearing from readers, who can contact her through her website, lisachilds.com, or snail-mail address, PO Box 139, Marne, MI 49435.

CAST OF CHARACTERS

Special Agent Blaine Campbell—The FBI agent has a perfect record for apprehending bank robbers, but the hostage he rescues during a robbery distracts and captivates him with her beauty.

Maggie Jenkins—The assistant bank manager has a dead fiancé, a baby on the way, and bank robbers determined to kidnap or kill her, so she turns to Agent Campbell for protection but finds more.

Richard Hardy—The bank manager may only be acting incompetent in order to cover his involvement in the robberies.

Susan Iverson—The bank teller has taken advantage of Maggie's kindness and might be using Maggie now to cover up her own crimes.

Andy Doremire—Maggie's dead fiancé might not be dead after all, if his father is telling the truth about seeing him.

Dustin Doremire—He's convinced his son is still alive and that he'll take Maggie's baby away from her—is he delusional or right?

Mark Doremire—Andy's brother might keep checking on Maggie just because he promised his brother he would take care of her, but his own wife thinks he has other motives.

Tammy Doremire—The woman is jealous of her husband's interest in Maggie—so much so that she might want to remove the threat to her marriage.

Chapter One

Gunshots erupted like a bomb blast, nearly shaking the walls of the glass-and-metal building. Through the wide windows and clear doors, Special Agent Blaine Campbell could easily assess the situation from the parking lot. Five suspects, wearing zombie masks and long black trench coats, fired automatic weapons inside the bank. Customers and employees cowered on the floor—all except for the uniform-clad bank security officer.

Blaine had already reported the robbery in progress and had been advised to wait for backup. He wasn't a fool; he could see that he was easily outgunned since he carried only his Glock and an extra clip.

But he left the driver's door hanging open on his rental car and ran across the parking lot crowded with customers' cars. How many potential hostages were inside that bank? How many potential casualties were there, with the way the robbers were firing those automatic weapons? Blaine couldn't wait for help—not when so many innocent people were in danger.

Ducking low, he shoved open the doors and burst into the bank lobby. "FBI!" he called out to calm the fears of the screaming and crying people.

But his entrance incited the robbers. Glass shattered behind him, as bullets whizzed over his head and through the windows, falling like rain over the customers lying faces down on the tile floor. The interior walls, which were glass partitions separating the offices from the main lobby, shattered, as well.

More people screamed and sobbed.

Blaine took cover behind one of the cement-and-steel pillars that held up the high ceiling of the modern building. He held out his hand, advising the customers to stay down as he surveyed them. Except for some cuts from the flying glass, nobody looked mortally wounded. None of the shots had hit anyone. Yet.

"Campbell," the security guard called out from behind another pillar. "You picked the right time to show up." The older man, who was also a friend, had called him here with suspicions that the bank was going to be robbed. Obviously Blaine's former boot-camp drill instructor's instincts were as sharp as ever. He had been right—except about Blaine.

He was too late. The robbers already carried bags overflowing with cash. If only he'd arrived earlier, before they'd gotten what they wanted...

He couldn't arrest them all on his own.

"Stay down!" one of the robbers yelled, as he fired his automatic rifle again.

A woman cried out as another robber tangled a gloved hand in her dark hair and pulled her up from the floor. She was close to one of the wrecked offices, so maybe she worked for the bank or had been meeting with one of the bank officers. She turned toward Blaine, her eyes wide with fear as if beseeching him for help.

But before he could take aim on the robber holding her, the security guard, armed only with a small-caliber handgun, stepped from behind his pillar. "Let her go!" Daryl Williams shouted as he fired at them.

"Sarge, get down," Blaine shouted.

But his advice came too late as a bullet struck the security guard's chest and blood spread across his gray uniform. The woman shrieked—either in reaction to Sarge getting shot or because she was afraid she might be next.

Blaine cursed, stepped out from behind the pillar and fired frantically back. One of the mask-wearing bank robbers spun around, as if Blaine had struck him. But he probably wore a bulletproof vest because he didn't drop to the floor as the guard had. Instead the robber hurried toward the back of the bank with the other zombies. One of them dragged along that terrified young woman. But now she stared back at Sarge instead of Blaine, her gaze full of fear and concern for the fallen security guard. Blaine scrambled over to his friend's side. The man wore his iron-gray hair in a military cut. He may have retired from the service, but he was still a soldier. "Hang in there, Sarge."

"Assist…assist." Daryl Williams tried to speak through the blood gurgling out of his mouth.

"I already called it in when I pulled up and heard the shots. Help is coming," Blaine promised, even though they both knew it would be too late.

Williams weakly shook his head. "Assist…manager…"

"The hostage?"

Daryl nodded even as his eyes rolled back into his head. He was gone.

And so was the woman. Of course Sergeant Williams would want Blaine to rescue her—the civilian. Remembering the stark fear on her pale face, Blaine snapped into action and hurried toward the back of the bank. Alarms wailed and lights flashed as the security door stood open to an alley. If it closed, he wouldn't be able to open it again. That must have been why the robbers had taken their hostage out the back, so she could open the security door for them. But why not leave her? Why take her along?

Blaine caught the door before it swung shut and pointed his gun into the alley. Bullets chiseled chips off the brick around the door as the bank robbers fired at him. If they had a getaway car parked in the alley, they obviously hadn't driven it away yet. He couldn't let them leave with the hostage or else nobody would probably ever see the young woman again. He had barely seen her long enough to give a description beyond dark hair and eyes.

Blaine risked a glance through the crack of the door and more bullets pinged off the steel. But he caught a glimpse of white metal—a van—as the side door opened. Another door slammed. The driver's? He couldn't let them get the hostage inside the vehicle, so he threw the bank door all the way open and burst into the alley. A shot struck him in the chest, but he kept going despite the impact of the bullet hitting his vest.

After his honorable discharge from active duty, he had thought the last thing he would miss was the helmet. He had hated the weight and the heat of it. But he could actually use one now—to protect himself from a head shot. More bullets struck his vest.

He returned fire, his shots glancing off the side of the van before one shattered the glass of the driver's window. Hopefully he'd struck the son of a bitch. But he didn't wait to find out; instead, he reached out for the hostage that one of the damn zombie robbers was pulling through the open side door. He caught the young woman's arm and jerked her backward as he fired into the van. The engine revved, and the vehicle burst forward, tires squealing.

But just in case the occupants fired back at them, he pushed the hostage to the ground and covered the young woman with his body. And that was when he realized she wasn't just terrified for herself but probably also for the child she carried.

She was pregnant.

The van kept going, but someone fired out the open back doors of it. And more bullets struck him, stealing his breath.

MAGGIE JENKINS'S THROAT was raw and her voice hoarse from screaming, but even though the robbers—dressed in those horrible zombie costumes—were gone, she wanted to scream again. She didn't want to scream out of fear for herself but for the man who lay on top of her. His body had gone limp as the breath left it.

He had been shot so many times. But he'd kept coming to her rescue like a golden-haired superhero. And then he'd covered her body with his, taking more shots to his back.

He had to be dead. Why had he interrupted the robbery in progress and risked his own life? He had claimed to be an FBI agent, but why would he have been alone? Why wouldn't he have waited for more agents and for local backup before bursting into the bank?

"Please, please be alive," she murmured, her voice no louder than a whisper. She grasped his shoulders—his impossibly wide shoulders—and eased him back. Something cold and metallic hung from his neck and pressed against her chest. A badge.

So he really was a lawman. But how had he known the bank was being robbed? When the robbers rushed the bank, she hadn't had the time or the nerve to push the silent alarm beneath her desk before bullets had shattered the glass walls of her office.

Maybe one of the tellers or Mr. Hardy, the bank manager, had pushed an alarm. Whatever the FBI agent had driven to the bank hadn't had sirens or lights. She hadn't even known he was there until he pushed open the lobby doors. But, then again, she had hardly been able to hear anything over all of those gunshots. Her ears rang from the deafening noise.

But now she heard his gasp as he caught his breath again. He stared down at her, his face so close that she picked up on all the nuances in his eyes. They were a deep green with flecks of gold that made them glitter. His body, long and muscular, tensed against hers. He moved the hand that was not holding his weapon to the asphalt and pushed up, levering himself off her.

"I'm sorry," he said.

He was apologizing to her? For what? Saving her life? Maybe shock had settled in, or maybe his good looks and his concern had struck her dumb. Usually she wasn't silent; usually people complained that she talked too much.

"Are you all right?" he asked.

Her hands covered her stomach, and something shifted beneath her palm. She sighed with relief that her baby was moving, flailing his tiny fists and kicking his tiny feet as if trying to fight off his mother's attackers.

But it was too late. This man had already fought them off for her. Of course her baby shouldn't be fighting to protect her; it was Maggie's job to protect him or her…

"Are you all right?" the man asked again. He slid his gun into a holster beneath his arm, and then he lifted her from the ground as easily as if she were half her size.

"How are you alive?" she asked in wonder.

He reached for his shirt and tore the buttons loose. The blue cotton parted to reveal a black vest. The badge swung back against it.

She was no longer close enough to read all the smaller print, but she identified the big brass-colored letters. "You really are an FBI agent? I thought you just said that to scare the robbers."

And she'd thought he had been a little crazy to try that when the robbers had had bigger guns than his. But maybe announcing his presence had scared the robbers into leaving quickly because they'd worried that backup would come.

Where was it, though?

"I'm Special Agent Blaine Campbell," he introduced himself.

"How did you get here so quickly?" she asked, still not entirely convinced that he wasn't a superhero. "How did you know the bank was being robbed?"

He shook his head and turned back to the building. "I didn't know that it was being robbed today. Sarge—Daryl Williams—called me a few days ago with concerns."

She gasped as she relived the security guard getting shot, flinching at the sound of the shot, at the image of him falling. He hadn't been wearing a vest, but he'd stepped out from behind that pillar anyway—undoubtedly to save her. "Is Sarge okay?"

The agent shook his head again, but he didn't speak, as if too overwhelmed for words. He had called Mr. Williams *Sarge*, so he must have known him well. Maybe Mr. Williams had once been his drill instructor, as he had been her fiancé's six years ago. The older man worked only part-time at the bank for something to do since he retired from the military.

If only he hadn't been there today…

If only he hadn't tried to save her…

The tears that had been burning her eyes brimmed over and began to slide down her face. She had just lost her fiancé a few months ago, and now she had lost another connection to him because Sarge had really known him. Not only had he trained him, but he'd also kept in touch with Andy over the years. He'd worried about him. He'd known that Andy shouldn't have joined the Marines; he hadn't been strong enough—physically or emotionally—to handle it. He had barely survived his first two deployments, and he had died on the first day of his last one.

Sarge had come for Andy's funeral and never left—intent on taking care of Maggie and her unborn baby since Andy was now unable to.

Strong arms wrapped around her, offering comfort when she suspected he needed it himself. Blaine Campbell had lost a man he'd obviously respected and cared about. So she hugged him back, clinging to him—until tires squealed and the back door of the bank burst open to the alley.

Guns cocked and voices shouted, "Get down! Get down!"

Fear filled her that the robbers had returned. She squeezed her eyes shut. She couldn't look at them again, couldn't see those horrific zombie costumes again. When she and Andy had been in middle school, his older brother had sneaked them into an R-rated zombie movie, and she'd been terrified of them ever since, even to the point where she didn't go to Halloween parties and even hid in the dark so no trick-or-treaters would come to her door.

But they kept coming to her.

Had they returned to make certain she and the agent were dead?

Chapter Two

"Agent Campbell," Blaine identified himself to the state troopers who'd drawn their weapons on him.

While he respected local law enforcement, especially troopers since his oldest sister was one in Michigan, he had met some unqualified officers over the years. So the gun barrels pointing at him and the woman next to him made him nervous. But he refused to get down or allow the pregnant woman to drop to the pavement again, either.

She had already been roughed up enough; her light gray suit was smudged with grease and oil from the alley. Her legs were scraped from connecting with the asphalt earlier. Had he done that when he'd shoved her down? Had he hurt her?

She had also lost a shoe—either in the bank or maybe in the van from which Blaine had pulled her, so she was unsteady on her feet. Or maybe her trembling wasn't because her balance was off but because she was in shock. He kept a hand on her arm, so that she didn't stumble and fall. But she needed more help than a hand to steady her.

"The bank robbers have already left in a white panel van," he continued. "The driver's-side window is broken and the rear taillights have been shot out." He read off the license plate number he'd memorized, as well.

One of the officers pressed the radio on his lapel and called in an APB on the vehicle. "What else can you tell us about the suspects, Agent Campbell?"

Fighting back the grief that threatened to overwhelm him, he replied, "One of them shot the security guard."

"We already have paramedics inside the bank," another officer told him. "They're treating the wounded."

They were too late to help Sarge. The man had died in his arms—his final words urging Blaine to save the assistant bank manager.

"You should have them check out Mrs….?" He turned to the young woman, waiting for her to supply her name. She hadn't offered it when he'd introduced himself earlier.

"Miss," she corrected him, almost absentmindedly. Her dark eyes seemed unfocused, as if she were dazed. "Maggie Jenkins…"

She was single. Now he allowed himself to notice how pretty she was. Her brown hair was long and curly and tangled around her shoulders. Her eyes were wide and heavily lashed. She was unmarried, but she probably wasn't single—not with her being as pretty as she was.

"The paramedics need to check out Miss Jenkins," he told the troopers. "The bank robbers were trying to take her hostage. She could have been hurt." But he might have been the one who'd done it when he had knocked her onto the hard asphalt of the alley.

"She should probably be taken to the hospital," he added. For an ultrasound to check out the well-being of her unborn child, too. But he didn't want to say it out loud and frighten her. The young woman had already been through enough.

The officer pressed his radio again and asked paramedics to come around to the back of the bank. They arrived quickly, backing the ambulance down the alley. A female paramedic pushed a stretcher out the doors and rolled it toward them.

But Miss Jenkins shook her head, refusing treatment. "What about Mr. Williams?" she asked. "He needs your help more than I do."

The paramedic just stared at her.

"The security guard," Miss Jenkins said. "One of the robbers shot him." Her already rough voice squeaked with emotion. "Will he be all right?"

The paramedic hesitated before shaking her head.

Tears spilled from Miss Jenkins's eyes again, trailing down her smooth face. She had cared about Sarge. But Blaine didn't think they could have worked together that long. Sarge had retired from the military only a few short months ago.

Blaine wanted to hold her again, to comfort her as he had earlier. Or had she comforted him? Her arms had slid around him, her curves soft and warm against him. He resisted the urge to reach for her, and instead he released her arm.

"Go with the paramedic," he said. "Let her check you out."

Blaine had questions for the assistant bank manager—so many questions. But his questions would wait until she was physically well enough to answer them.

The troopers immediately began to question Blaine. He had to explain his presence and about Sarge—even while tears of loss stung his eyes. He blinked them back, knowing his former drill instructor would have kicked his butt if he showed any weakness. Sarge had taught all his recruits that a good marine—a strong marine—controlled his emotions. Blaine had already learned that before boot camp, though.

"Why did the security guard call you?" one of the troopers asked.

"I just transferred to the Chicago Bureau office to take over the investigation of the robbers who've been hitting banks in Illinois, Michigan and Indiana." Bank robberies were his specialty. He had a perfect record; no bank robbery he had investigated had gone unsolved, no bank robber unapprehended.

Of course, some robbers were sloppy and desperate and easily caught. Blaine already knew that this group of them—in their trench coats and zombie masks—were not sloppy or desperate. And, therefore, they would not be easily caught. But he would damn well catch them.

For Sarge…

"You think those robberies are related to this one?" the trooper asked.

"I can't make a determination yet." Because he hadn't had a chance to go to the office; his flight had landed only hours ago. But ever since Sarge's call, the urgency in the man's voice had haunted Blaine and made him come here first—with his suitcase in the trunk of a rental car. "I need more information."

And he didn't want to give up too much information to the troopers before he'd verified his facts. He needed to check in with the Bureau, but he couldn't leave the scene yet.

He couldn't leave Maggie Jenkins.

He turned back to where the paramedic had helped her into the back of the first-responder rig. A man in a suit was standing outside the doors, talking to her. He'd come through the back door of the bank, so the troopers must have cleared him.

Blaine recognized him as one of the people who'd been lying on the floor, cowering from the robbers. Instead of checking on her, the man appeared to be questioning her—the way Blaine wanted to. But he wasn't certain she had any more information than he did.

He just wanted to make sure she was all right—that his rescue hadn't done her more harm than being taken hostage had.

Maggie was finally alone. Mr. Hardy, the bank manager, had gone back inside the damaged building to call the corporate headquarters, as she had told him to do. At thirty, he was young and inexperienced for his position, so he had no idea what to do or how to manage after a robbery.

Unfortunately, Maggie did.

She trembled—not with cold or even with fear. She hadn't felt that until the bullet had struck Sarge, and he had dropped to the floor. Before that, when the gunmen had burst into the lobby wearing those masks and trench coats, she had been too stunned to feel anything at all.

Usually just the sight of those gruesome masks would have filled her with terror, as they had ever since Andy and Mark had sneaked her into that violent horror movie. She'd had nightmares for years over it. But for the past few months she'd been having new nightmares. And while they'd still been about zombies, they hadn't been movie actors—they'd been about *these* zombies.

"I can't believe it," she murmured to herself. "I can't believe it happened. Again…"

And it was that disbelief that had overwhelmed her fear—until Sarge had been shot.

"Are you all right?" a deep voice asked.

Startled, she tensed. It wasn't one of the paramedics. Their voices were higher and less…commanding. Agent Campbell commanded attention and respect and control.

He had taken over the moment he'd burst into the bank with his weapon drawn. He had taken over and saved her from whatever the bank robbers had planned for her. And he'd taken over the investigation from the state troopers more easily.

She nodded. "I'm okay," she assured him, worried that he might think she was losing it. "I always talk to myself. My parents claim I came out talking and never shut up…" But as she chattered, her teeth began to chatter, too, snapping together as her jaw trembled.

The FBI agent lifted the blanket a paramedic had put around her and he wrapped it more tightly—as if he were swaddling a baby. She had taken a class and swaddled a doll, but she hadn't done it nearly as well as he had. Maybe he had children of his own. She glanced down at his hands—his big, strong hands—but they were bare of any rings. Not every married man wore one, though. Her face heated with embarrassment that she'd even looked. His marital status should have been the last thing on her mind.

"Thank you," she said. "I'm fine, really…" But it wasn't cold out. Why was she so deeply chilled that even her bones felt cold? "I can go back inside the bank and help Mr. Hardy—"

"The bank manager," he said.

She'd noticed that he had stopped Mr. Hardy before letting him back inside the bank. And he'd questioned him. She doubted the young manager had been able to provide many answers.

"Yes," she said. "I need to go back inside and help him close up the bank and take inventory for corporate. There's so much to do…" There always was, after a robbery.

"You need to go to the hospital and get checked out,"

Agent Campbell said as he waved over the paramedic. "You should have already taken her."

"She wanted to talk to you first," the female paramedic replied. She'd told Maggie that she wouldn't mind talking to the agent herself, and her male partner had scoffed at her lack of professionalism.

Maggie hadn't intended to go to the hospital at all—not when there was so much to do inside the bank. And Sarge...

Was he still inside?

She shuddered, then shivered harder. And the baby shifted inside her, kicking her ribs. She flinched and nodded. "Maybe I should get checked out..."

For the baby. She had to protect her baby. She had nearly three months left of her pregnancy—three months to keep her unborn child safe. She hadn't realized how hard that might be.

"My questions can wait," the FBI agent told her, "until you've been thoroughly checked out." He turned toward the paramedics. "Which hospital will you take her to?"

"Med West," the woman paramedic replied. "You can ride along and question her in the back of the rig."

Maggie stilled her trembling as she waited for his reply. She wanted him to agree; she felt safer with him close. She felt safe in his arms...

And after what had happened—again—she would have doubted she would ever feel safe. Anywhere.

"Agent Campbell," one of the officers called out to him. He didn't pull his gaze from her, his green eyes intense on her face. The officer continued anyway. "We located the van."

That got the agent's attention; he turned away from her. "And the robbers?"

The officer shrugged. "We don't know if there's anyone inside. Nobody's approached it yet."

Maggie struggled free of the blanket and grabbed the agent's arm—even though she knew she couldn't stop him. He was going.

"Be careful," she advised him.

She had told Andy the same thing when he had left her last, but he hadn't listened to her. She hoped Agent Campbell did. Or the next time the robbers' bullets might miss his vest and hit somewhere else instead.

Agent Campbell barely spared her a nod before heading off with the state troopers. He had been lucky during his first confrontation with the thieves, but Andy had been lucky, too, during his first two deployments.

Eventually, though, luck ran out…

HIS GUN STEADY in one hand, Blaine slid open the side door with the other. But the van was empty. The robbers had ditched it between Dumpsters at the end of an alley.

"This vehicle was reported stolen three days ago," one of the troopers informed him.

Either they'd stolen it themselves or picked it up from someone who dealt in stolen vehicles. It was a lead that Blaine could follow. Maybe someone had witnessed the theft.

They must have exchanged the van for another vehicle they had stashed close to the bank. They'd had to move quickly, though, so they hadn't taken time to wipe down the van.

They had left behind forensic evidence. Blaine could see some of it now. Fibers from their clothes. Hair—either from their masks or their own. And blood. It could have been fake; they'd had some on their gruesome disguises. But that hadn't looked like this.

This blood was smeared and drying already into dark pools.

"You hit one of them?" a trooper asked.

He hoped he'd hit the one who'd killed Sarge. "I fired at them, but I thought they were wearing vests."

"You must be a good shot," the trooper replied.

More likely he had gotten off a lucky shot. He was fortunate one of them hadn't done the same. If they hadn't been worried that he had backup coming, they probably would have killed him the way they had Sarge.

Blaine sighed. "But the suspect wasn't hurt so badly that he couldn't get away." As they had all gotten away. But at least one of them had not been unscathed.

"Put out an APB that one of the suspects might be seeking medical treatment for a gunshot wound," Blaine said, "at a hospital or doctor's office or med center. Hell, don't rule out a vet clinic. These guys will not want the wound getting reported." And doctors were legally obligated to report gunshot wounds.

So he wouldn't worry that he had sent Maggie Jenkins off to the hospital in the back of that ambulance. He wouldn't worry that one of the men who had tried to abduct her earlier might get a chance to try again.

Again...

What had she been muttering when he'd walked up to the ambulance? Her already soft voice had been strained from screaming, so he'd struggled to hear, let alone understand, her words. But she'd murmured something about not believing that it had happened. Again...

Had Maggie Jenkins been the victim of a bank robbery before?

The same bank robbers?

Hell, Blaine was worried now. Not just that she might be in danger but that he might have let the best lead to the robbers ride away. Had he let her big, dark eyes and her fear and vulnerability influence his opinion of her?

What if Maggie Jenkins hadn't been a hostage but a coconspirator?

Maybe Sarge hadn't been trying to tell him to rescue the assistant bank manager. Maybe he had been trying to tell Blaine to catch her.

Chapter Three

Maggie pressed her palms over the hospital gown covering her belly and tried to soothe the child moving inside her. He kept kicking, as though he was still fighting. "I'm sorry, baby," she said. "I know Mama's not doing a very good job of keeping you safe."

But she'd tried.

Why was it that danger kept finding her? She had already changed jobs, or at least locations, but she couldn't afford to quit. Maybe she should have married Andy one of the times he had suggested it. They had been together since middle school, and she'd loved him. But she hadn't been *in* love with him.

"I'm sorry," she said again. But this time she was talking to Andy.

She should have told him the truth, but he'd enlisted right out of high school and she hadn't wanted to be the heartless girlfriend who wrote the Dear John letter. And when he'd come home on leave, she had been so happy to see him—so happy to have her best friend back—that she hadn't wanted to risk losing that friendship.

But eventually she had lost him—to a roadside bomb in Afghanistan. Tears stung her eyes and tickled her nose, but she drew in a shaky breath and steadied herself. She had to be strong—for her baby. Since he had already lost his father, he needed her twice as much.

A hand drew back the curtain of Maggie's corner of the emergency department. The young physician's assistant who'd talked to her earlier smiled reassuringly. "I had a doctor and a radiologist review the ultrasound," the PA said, "and we all agree that your baby is fine."

Maggie released her breath as a sigh of relief. "That's great."

"You, on the other hand, have some bumps and bruises, and your blood pressure is a little high," the PA continued. "So you need to be careful and take better care of yourself."

She nodded in agreement. Not that she hadn't been trying. That had been the whole point of her new job—less stress. But Mr. Hardy wasn't as competent as the manager at the previous branch where she'd worked. And the zombie bank robbers had hit the new bank anyway.

Maybe she would have been safer had she stayed where she'd been. "I will take better care of myself and the baby," Maggie vowed. "Do you know what I'm having?" She had had an ultrasound earlier in her pregnancy, but it had been too soon to tell the gender.

The young woman shook her head. "I wasn't able to tell."

Or she probably would have pointed it out then.

"But maybe the radiologist had an idea." The young woman's face flushed as she glanced down at the notes. "I'm sorry," she said. "I hadn't realized that you'd been at the bank that was robbed and that paramedics had brought you from the scene."

"That's fine," Maggie said. "I should have told you myself." But she hadn't wanted to talk about it—to remember what it had been like to see those gruesome masks again and to watch as one of them killed Sarge. She shuddered.

"Of course your blood pressure would be elevated," the PA continued. "You must have been terrified."

She had been until the FBI agent had saved her. Where was he? He was supposed to come to the hospital to interview her. Hadn't Agent Campbell survived his second run-in with the bank robbers?

"I'll be okay," she assured the physician's assistant. She had survived. Again. Daryl Williams hadn't been as fortunate—because of her. Maybe Agent Campbell hadn't survived, either.

The young woman nodded. "Considering what you've been through, you're doing very well. But I would follow up with your obstetrician tomorrow and make sure your blood pressure goes down."

"I will do that," Maggie promised. She was taking no chances with her pregnancy. She had already lost the baby's father; she wouldn't lose his baby, too.

"You can get dressed now." The young woman passed over some papers. "Here is your release and an ultrasound picture. There isn't any way of telling his or her gender yet."

Maggie stared down at the photo. She had seen her baby on the ultrasound screen this time and the previous time she'd had one. But this was the first photo she'd been given to keep—probably because he looked like a baby now and not a peanut. He or she was curled up on his or her side, and the little mouth was open. She smiled as she remembered her mother claiming that Maggie's mouth had been open during every ultrasound. She'd been talking even before she'd been born.

"Thank you," she told the PA. But she didn't look up. She couldn't take her gaze from the amazing photo of her baby. The child had already survived so much: the loss of a parent and two bank robberies.

"Good luck, Ms. Jenkins," the young woman replied as she pulled the curtain closed again.

Maggie's smile slid off her lips. She was going to need luck to make it safely through her pregnancy and deliver a healthy baby. He was fine now. And she would do everything within her power to keep him that way.

She dressed quickly so that she could pick up and study the picture again. Maybe she should wait for the FBI agent—to make certain that he was all right. It wasn't as if she could leave anyway. Her purse was back at the bank, so she didn't have any money to pay for a cab. And with Mr. Hardy busy with corporate, the only other person she could have called at the bank to bring it to her was dead.

Sarge…

If only he hadn't stepped out from behind that pillar…

If only he hadn't tried to save her…

Tears blurred her vision, but she blinked them back to focus on the baby picture again. She needed to focus on him or her, needed to keep him or her healthy and safe. The baby was her priority.

She would have to find a phone she could use and call a friend to pick her up. But she didn't really know anyone here in this suburb of Chicago. She hadn't known anyone but Sarge. After the bank where she'd previously worked had been robbed, she had transferred to the branch where Sarge worked—thinking she would feel safer with him there. But the danger had followed her and claimed his life—cruelly cutting his retirement short. The tears threatened again, but she fought them. Sobbing would not help her blood pressure.

The curtain moved as a gloved hand pulled it back.

"I'm sorry," she said, feeling guilty for taking up the

area. "I realize you probably need the bed for someone else..." For someone who actually needed medical attention. "I'm all ready to leave." She just needed someone to pick her up. "I can wait in the lobby."

Nobody said anything, though. But she could feel them standing there, watching her. So then she looked up, and her heart began to pound frantically as she stared into the creepy face of one of those horrible zombie masks. It was her nightmare come to life again.

She would have screamed but for the gun barrel pointing directly at her. She already knew that these people had no compunction about killing. They had already killed once and that had been because Sarge had been trying to save her. She couldn't scream and risk someone else getting hurt again. The only reason they would have tracked her down at the hospital was to kill again.

To kill *her*...

BLAINE CURSED HIMSELF as he flipped screens on his tablet. The Bureau had forwarded him the case file for the bank robberies.

Now he knew exactly what Maggie had been muttering in the back of the ambulance—because it had happened again. A different bank. A different city. But the same witness.

Maggie Jenkins had been robbed before—a couple of months ago—at another bank where she'd been working as an assistant manager. What were the odds that the same robbers, wearing zombie masks and black trench coats, would track her down at another bank in another city? Maybe it was a coincidence, but in his years with the Bureau, Blaine had found few true coincidences.

It was more likely that they knew her. And if they knew her, she knew them. He'd had a lot of questions for

Maggie Jenkins before; now he had even more. And he wouldn't let her tear-damp dark eyes or her sweet vulnerability distract him again.

He dropped the tablet onto the passenger seat and threw open the driver's door. After clicking the locks, he hurried across the parking lot to the hospital. He sidestepped through the automatic doors before they were fully open and flashed his badge at the security guard standing inside the doors. "I'm looking for a witness who was brought here from a bank-robbery scene. Maggie Jenkins."

After waving him through the blinking, beeping metal detector, the guard pointed toward the emergency-department desk. Blaine showed his badge to the receptionist. "I need to talk to Maggie Jenkins—from the bank robbery."

The older woman stared at his badge before nodding. "Nyla can show you where she is."

A young nurse stepped from behind the desk and pushed open swinging doors. "Ms. Jenkins is behind the last curtain on the left."

He followed the woman's directions, past a long row of pulled curtains, and he pulled aside the very last curtain on the left. The bed was empty but for a black-and-white photo. Maggie was gone. He picked up the photo and recognized it as an ultrasound picture. His older sisters had shown him a few over the past ten years. He'd thought they looked like Rorschach tests. They had all prized them.

No matter what her involvement was in the robberies, Maggie Jenkins wouldn't have willingly left that photo behind. He reached for his holster and whirled around to the nurse who'd followed him. "She's gone."

Unconcerned, the young woman shrugged. "She was cleared to get dressed and leave."

"She came by ambulance and didn't have her purse," he said. "She couldn't have left on her own." Not with no car and no money for a cab. At the very least, she would have had to call someone to pick her up. But then, why wouldn't she have taken the ultrasound photo with her? "Did you see anyone come back here?"

Metal scraped against metal as another curtain was tugged back, its rings scraping along the rod. A little girl, propped against pillows in a bed, peered out at Blaine. "The monster came for her."

His skin chilled as dread chased over him. "What monster?"

An older woman, probably the little girl's mother, was sitting in a chair next to the bed. With a slight smile, she shook her head. "It wasn't a monster. Just someone wearing a silly Halloween mask."

"But it's not Halloween," the little girl said, as if she suspected her mother was lying and that the monster was very real.

Blaine was worried that the monster was real, too. "Was it a zombie mask that the person was wearing?"

The woman shrugged. "I don't know."

But the little girl's already pale face grew even paler with fear as she slowly nodded. "It was a really creepy zombie. He was wearing a long black coat."

Blaine's dread spread the chill throughout him. He bit back a curse. One of the robbers had tracked her down at the hospital?

The woman shrugged again. "He put his fingers to his lips, so that we wouldn't say anything. He was just playing a joke."

Apparently the woman hadn't seen any of the news coverage about the zombie robbers.

The nurse shook her head in vigorous denial of the

little girl's claim. "I didn't see anyone dressed like that in this area, and the security guard wouldn't have let him through the front doors."

"What about the back doors?" he asked. "Could someone have come in another way?"

"Only employees can," the nurse replied.

He doubted that employees had to go through a metal detector the way visitors had to. "Show me."

The nurse stepped around the curtain to show Blaine another set of double doors on that end of the emergency department—just a few feet from where Maggie had been. If the robber had come through those doors, no one would have seen him but Maggie and apparently the little girl next to her. He wouldn't have gone through security if he'd come in the employee entrance. The nurse had to swipe her ID card to open those doors. They swung into an empty corridor.

"How would someone get to the parking lot from here?" he asked.

With a sigh of exasperation, as if he was wasting her time, she turned left and continued down the corridor to a couple of single doors. "The locker rooms have doors to a back hallway that leads to the employee parking lot," she said in anticipation of his next questions. "But it's too soon for a shift change, so nobody's back here now."

But a noise emanated from behind one of the doors. A thump. And then a scream pierced the air. Blaine grabbed the nurse's ID badge and swiped it through the lock. As he pushed open the door, shots rang out. A bullet struck him—in the vest over his heart. The force of it knocked him against the door and forced the breath from his lungs.

The nurse cried and ran back down the corridor. Then another scream rang out—from Maggie Jenkins. She had fallen to her knees. But the bank robber had a gloved hand in her hair, trying to pull her up—trying to drag her to that door at the back of the locker room—the door that would lead to the employee parking lot.

How did he know where to take her? How did he have the access badge to do it? He must either be an employee of the hospital or he knew an employee very well.

Ignoring the pain she must have been in from that hand in her hair, Maggie wriggled and reached as she continued to scream for help. But she didn't wait for Blaine's help. She tried to help herself. She grabbed at the benches between the rows of lockers and at the lockers, too, as she tried to prevent the robber from dragging her off. She flailed her arms and kicked, too, desperately trying to fight off her attacker. But then the gun barrel swung toward her face and she froze.

Was the robber just trying to scare her into cooperating? Or did he intend to kill her right here, in front of Blaine?

Chapter Four

Maggie couldn't breathe; she couldn't move. She couldn't do anything but stare down the barrel of the gun that had been shoved in her face.

Agent Campbell had stepped inside the room, but then a shot had slammed him back against the door. Wasn't he wearing his vest anymore? Was he hurt?

Or worse?

She wanted to look, but she was frozen with fear. Because she was about to be *worse*, too. With the barrel so close to her face, there was no way the bullet could miss her head. She was about to die.

In her peripheral vision, she was aware of the gloved finger pressing on the trigger. And she heard the shot. It exploded in the room, shattering the silence and deafening her. But she felt no pain. Neither did she fall. She still couldn't move. Apparently she couldn't feel, either.

But the gun moved away from her face. With a dull thud, it dropped to the floor. And the robber fell, too, backward over one of the benches in what appeared to be the employee locker room.

The robber had forced her to be quiet while they'd been in Emergency—because he'd kept the barrel of the gun tight against her belly. He would have killed her baby if she'd called out for help. But when he'd brought her to this locker room, he'd had to move the gun away to swipe the badge. And so, as the doors were closing behind them, she'd risked calling out.

But she hadn't expected Agent Campbell to come to her aid again. He must have recovered from the shot that had knocked him back because now he started forward again, toward the robber. But he stopped to kick away the gun, and the robber vaulted to his feet. He picked up one of the benches and hurled it at the FBI agent. It knocked Blaine Campbell back—into Maggie.

She fell against the lockers, the back of her head striking the metal so hard that spots danced before her eyes. Her vision blurred. Then her legs, already shaking with her fear, folded under her, and she slid down to the floor.

While the bench had knocked over the agent, he hadn't lost his grip on his gun. And he fired it again at the robber. The man flinched at the impact of the bullet. But like the agent, he must have worn a vest because the shot didn't stop him. But he didn't fight anymore. Instead he turned and ran.

"Stop!" the agent yelled.

But the man in the zombie mask didn't listen, or at least he didn't heed the command in Agent Campbell's voice as everyone else had. He pushed open the back door with such force that metal clanged as it struck the outside wall. Then the man ran through that open door.

Campbell jumped up, but instead of heading off in pursuit of the robber, he turned back to her and asked, "Are you all right?"

The gunfire echoed in her ears yet, so his deep voice sounded far away. She couldn't focus on it; she couldn't focus on him, either.

But his handsome face came closer as he dropped to

his knees in front of her. His green eyes full of concern and intensity, he asked, "Maggie, are you all right?"

No. She couldn't speak, and she was usually never at a loss for words. Her heart kept racing even though the robber and his gun were no longer threatening her. In fact, the more she stared into the agent's eyes, the faster her heart beat. The green was so vibrant—like the first leaves on a tree in spring. Just as she had been unable to look anywhere but the barrel of the gun in her face, she couldn't look away from the agent's beautiful eyes.

"Maggie…" Fingers skimmed along her cheek. "Are you all right?"

She opened her mouth, but no words slipped out. Her pulse quickened, and her breath grew shallower— so shallow that she couldn't get any air. And then she couldn't see Agent Campbell any longer as her vision blurred and then blackened.

BLAINE SHOULD HAVE been in hot pursuit of the robber. He should have been firing shots and taking him down in the parking lot. Instead he was standing over a pregnant woman, waiting for her to regain consciousness. And as he waited, he drew in some deep breaths—hoping to ease the tightness in his chest.

The intern, who had come running, along with the security guards, when Blaine had yelled for medical help, assured him that she was fine. She and her baby were fine. She must have just hyperventilated. And with someone shooting at her, it was understandable—or so the intern had thought.

Blaine wasn't sure what to think. Had she really passed out? Or had she only staged a diversion so the robber could get away from him and those guards that nurse Nyla had called to the locker room?

But then, if Maggie was an accomplice, why had she fought the man so hard? Why had she looked so terrified?

His older sisters had pulled off drama well in their teens. They'd worked their parents to get what they wanted, so he'd seen some pretty good actresses work their manipulations up close and personal. But if Maggie Jenkins had been acting in the locker room, she surpassed his sisters.

"Who are you really, Maggie Jenkins?" he wondered aloud. Innocent victim or criminal mastermind?

Her thick, dark lashes fluttered against her cheeks, as if she'd heard him and his words had roused her to consciousness. She blinked and stared up at him, looking as dazed and shocked as she had when she'd fallen against the lockers.

When he'd inadvertently knocked her against them. A pang of guilt had him flinching, and he fisted his hands to keep them from reaching for her belly to check on the baby. It had been real to him even before he'd seen the picture, but now it was even more real.

"The doctor said you and your baby are not hurt," he assured her. And himself.

"Are you okay?" she asked, and her brown eyes softened with concern.

He shrugged off her worry. "I'm fine."

He would probably have a bruise where the bench had clipped his shoulder, but his physical well-being was the least of his concerns right now.

She stared up at him, her smooth brow furrowing slightly, as if she doubted his words. "Really?"

No. He was upset about Sarge. And he was frustrated as hell that he'd lost one of the leads to Sarge's killer—or maybe the actual killer himself—when the robber had run out the employee exit to the parking lot. But Blaine had another lead—one he didn't intend to let out of his sight.

"I'm worried about you," he admitted. For so many reasons…

She tensed and protectively splayed her hands over her belly. "You said the baby isn't hurt."

"The baby is fine," he assured her. "And so are you."

She stared up at him again, this time full of doubt.

So he added, "For now."

Despite the blanket covering her, she shivered at his foreboding tone.

"You're obviously in danger," he said, "since one of the robbers risked coming here to abduct you from the ER." Or had she called him? Had she wanted to be picked up before Blaine could question her further?

He needed to take her down to the Bureau, or at least the closest police department for an interrogation. But if he started treating her like a suspect, she might react like one and clam up or lawyer up. Maybe it was better if he let her continue to play the victim…

But her eyes—those big, dark eyes—didn't fill with tears this time. Instead her gaze hardened and she clenched her delicate jaw. Angrily she asked, "Why won't they leave me alone?"

"I'm not sure why you were tracked down at the hospital today," he replied.

Could it have been another coincidence? Could the robber have been here to get treatment for the gunshot wound Blaine had inflicted and then stumbled upon her?

But the robber hadn't seemed injured—especially since he'd had the strength to hurl the bench with such force at Blaine. And he'd been fighting with Maggie before that. Maybe he wasn't the injured robber, but had been bringing that one for treatment…

But where was that person?

He'd already lost so much blood in the van.

"Why did one of them come here?" she asked—the same question Blaine had been asking himself. "What do they want with *me*?"

That was another question Blaine had been asking himself. "Maybe you saw or heard something back at the bank," he suggested, "something that might give away the identity of one of them?"

She shook her head. "I couldn't see any of their faces. They wore those horrible masks…" And she shuddered.

"What about their voices?"

"Only one of them spoke at the bank," she said, "and I didn't recognize his voice."

Did the others not speak because she would have recognized one of their voices? And now he wondered about the father of her baby…

But wouldn't she have recognized him despite the disguise? Wouldn't she have recognized his build, his walk, any of his mannerisms? Or maybe she had but wasn't about to implicate him and possibly herself.

Blaine waited, hoping that she would voluntarily admit to having been robbed before. But if she'd been about to confess to anything, she was interrupted when the hospital security chief approached.

The chief was a woman—probably in her fifties, with short gray hair and a no-nonsense attitude. Blaine had been impressed when he'd spoken with her earlier when she'd joined her security guards in the locker room. She was furious that someone had brought a gun into the hospital and nearly abducted one of the patients.

"Agent Campbell," Mrs. Wright said. "As you requested, I have all the footage pulled up from the security cameras."

"Thank you," he said. "That was fast." Hopefully one of those cameras had caught the robber without his hideous disguise. But Blaine hesitated again.

"The security room is this way," Mrs. Wright said, making a gesture for him to follow her from the emergency department.

But he didn't want to leave Maggie Jenkins alone and unprotected. "Do you have a guard that you can post here with Ms. Jenkins?"

Mrs. Wright nodded. "Of course. The police are here now, too. Sergeant Torreson is waiting in the security room to meet with you."

He needed Sergeant Torreson posted by Maggie Jenkins's bed, so that nobody could get to her. And so that she couldn't get away before she finally and truthfully answered all his questions. "Is he the only officer?"

Because he really didn't want to use one of the security guards—not when the zombie robber had to either be an employee or be close friends with an employee. He couldn't trust anyone who worked for the hospital. Not a doctor, nurse or even a security guard…

Mrs. Wright gestured to where a young policeman stood near the nurse who'd brought Blaine back to the employee locker room. He wasn't sure if the man was interrogating or flirting with her, so he waved him over to Maggie's bedside. "I'm Agent Campbell."

"Yes, sir," the young man replied. "We're aware you're the FBI special agent in charge of the investigation into the bank robberies."

Blaine studied the kid's face, looking for the familiar signs of resentment from local law enforcement. But he detected nothing but respect. The tightness in his chest eased slightly. He had backup, and given how relentless the bank robbers were, he needed it.

Of course, he could have called in more agents. Immediately after the robbery, he'd checked in, and the Bureau chief had offered him more FBI resources. But

Blaine had thought the bank robbers gone—the immediate threat over—until he'd come to the hospital and nearly lost the witness. But was Maggie a witness or an accomplice?

"Officer, this is Maggie Jenkins, the woman who was nearly abducted," he introduced them. "I need you posted here to protect her until I come back."

"I'll be fine," Maggie said. "I'll be safe." But her hands trembled as she splayed them across her belly again. She was either afraid or nervous. "I'll be safe," she repeated, as if trying to convince herself.

"We can't be certain of that," Blaine said. After all, the robbers kept returning…for her.

She slowly nodded in agreement, and tears welled now in her dark eyes. The tightness returned to his chest. But, growing up with three older and very dramatic sisters, he should have been immune to tears—especially since Maggie actually looked more frustrated than sad. But something about the young woman affected him and brought out his protective instincts.

But maybe the person he needed to protect when it came to Maggie Jenkins was himself.

"Be vigilant," Blaine advised the young officer. "For some reason these guys keep coming after her." And he intended to find out that reason. But he suspected he could learn more from the footage than he could Maggie Jenkins. She obviously wasn't being forthcoming with him.

So he headed to the surveillance room. But his mind wasn't on the footage he watched or on the police sergeant's questions, either. The hospital was a busy one—with so many people coming and going that it wouldn't be easy to determine which one might have walked in as himself and emerged as a zombie robber.

That was the only footage in which he could positively identify the person—as he burst through the back door and ran across the employee parking lot. But he kept the disguise on even as he jumped into an idling vehicle.

The sergeant cursed. "These guys—with those damn silly Halloween masks—have hit two banks in my jurisdiction."

As the vehicle, another van, turned, the driver came into view of the camera. But they must have known that camera would be there because the driver wore one of those damn masks, too.

"I want you to review your employees," Blaine told the hospital security chief. "Find out who wasn't working today."

"The hospital has hundreds of full- and part-time employees," Mrs. Wright said. "That'll take some time."

"*Your* employees," Blaine said. "I want you to focus on the security staff." He was really glad that he hadn't left Maggie Jenkins in the protection of one of the hospital guards.

"You think it's one of my people?" Mrs. Wright asked— with all the resentment he usually confronted with local law enforcement.

He pointed toward the masked men. "They knew where the cameras are—they knew how to get a gun in and out. They were familiar with employee-only areas of the hospital."

"But…" The woman's argument sputtered out as she grimly accepted that he was right.

Blaine turned toward the police officer. "I'd like you to bring in more officers, Sergeant. And check out anyone on that footage who walked in carrying a bag or a suitcase—anything big enough to carry that disguise and a weapon."

The woman sighed. "There is a metal detector at the front door."

Blaine was well aware of that—since he'd had to have a security guard wave him through it. But he'd wanted the security chief to come on her own to the same realization that he had. It had to be one of her people. But that didn't mean another robber hadn't come through the front door—an injured one.

"It'll still take me some time," she said. "We have three shifts, and since we have some trouble with gangs in this area, we have several guards on staff."

"Check out ex-staff, too," Blaine suggested.

"I'll help you," the sergeant offered.

He wanted the robbers, as well. But he didn't want them as badly as Blaine did. One of them had killed his friend and former mentor. Blaine couldn't let them get away with that—with ending what should have been Sarge's golden years way too soon.

"I have one of your officers helping me now," Blaine told the sergeant. "He's guarding the hostage for me."

The sergeant winced. "That kid's a trainee and easily distracted."

Blaine cursed and rushed out of the security room. He had wasted too much time on footage that had revealed no clues when he should have been interrogating his only concrete lead. But when he returned to the emergency department, he found the young officer flirting with the nurse once again.

And he found the bed where he'd left Maggie Jenkins empty. She was gone. Either she'd been grabbed again, or she'd escaped…

Chapter Five

Even though they had left the hospital a while ago, Special Agent Campbell had yet to speak to her. He only spared her a glare as he drove. The man was furious with her. A muscle twitched along his jaw, and his gaze was hot and hard. Maggie found his anger nearly as intimidating as his devastating good looks. But she couldn't understand why he was mad at her. Unless...

His stare moved off her to focus on the road again. He hadn't said where he was taking her. She had foolishly just assumed it would be to her apartment. Now she wasn't so certain...

Her wrists were bare; he hadn't cuffed her. She sat in the passenger's seat next to him—not in the back. But was he arresting her?

"Do you think I'm involved in the robberies?" she asked. "Is that why you were so upset when you couldn't find me at the hospital?"

That muscle twitched in his cheek again. "When you were gone, I assumed the worst."

The worst to her would have been one of the robbers in the creepy zombie mask returning. But she wasn't convinced that Agent Campbell thought the same.

"Is that really what you thought?" she asked. "That

one of them had come back for me? Or had you thought that I'd taken off on my own?"

"I thought you were gone," he said, which didn't really answer her question. "And I had left that young officer to protect you..."

"I was only using the restroom," she reminded him. "And he couldn't go into the ladies' with me." She had stepped out of the room to raised voices in the ER. For a moment she'd feared that one of the robbers had returned... until she'd recognized the voices.

At first she had been touched that Agent Campbell had been concerned about her. But he hadn't been relieved that she was okay; he had stayed angry. Even after checking her out of the hospital and seeing her safely to his vehicle, he was still angry.

"You do suspect that I'm involved in the robberies," she said, answering her own question.

"Robberies?" he queried, his tone guarded. But then, everything about Special Agent Blaine Campbell was guarded and hard to read—except for the grief he'd felt over Sarge's death. It had been easy to see his pain.

"They've robbed more than one bank," she said. "But you know that..." Or the FBI wouldn't have taken over the case. She suspected he was also aware of something else, too. "You probably know that they robbed the other branch of this bank where I previously worked."

"And then they followed you to the bank where you're working now..." His tone was less guarded now and more suspicious.

Of her?

Her stomach pitched. She hadn't had morning sickness even in her first trimester, so that wasn't the problem. It was nerves. He obviously did suspect that she was involved in the robberies.

"They have robbed a lot of other banks that I haven't worked at," she pointed out.

"How do you know that?" he asked, as if she had somehow slipped up and implicated herself. "How do you know how many other banks have been robbed?"

"From the news," she said. "They've even made national broadcasts. And our corporate headquarters sends out email warnings about robberies at other branches or other banks in the area. So it was just a coincidence that they hit both banks where I've worked."

A horrible coincidence—that was what she'd been trying to tell herself since the robbers, in those grotesque disguises, had burst through the doors of the bank earlier that afternoon.

"They have robbed other banks," he agreed. "But you're the only hostage they've tried taking. They didn't abduct anyone from any other bank."

She shuddered. "That was just today…" They hadn't tried to take her last time; they'd only had her open the security door to the alley. Then they'd left.

"So what was different about today?" he asked.

"You." He was the first thing that came to mind. Actually, since he'd saved her from being kidnapped the first time, Special Agent Blaine Campbell—with his golden-blond hair and intense green eyes—hadn't left her mind. Then he'd saved her a second time…

That muscle twitched again in his cheek, which was beginning to grow dark with stubble a few shades darker than his blond hair. "I wasn't the only thing different about today."

She uttered a ragged sigh and blinked back the tears that threatened as she remembered what else had been different. "They killed Sarge."

"Until today they hadn't killed anyone," he said. "Do you know what that means?"

She shook her head. She didn't know how a person could take another life for any reason. That was why she hadn't been able to understand Andy's insistence on joining the military. He had always been so sensitive. He had never even hunted and had been inconsolable when he'd accidentally struck and killed a deer with his truck.

Agent Campbell answered his own question, his voice threatening. "It means that whoever has been helping them will face murder charges, as well."

So he didn't think she was only a thief; he thought she was a killer, too. Anger coursed through her. She was the one who was mad now.

"Sarge was my friend," she said. "And what today means to me is that I lost a friend. I thought it meant the same to you. I thought you knew him and cared about him."

His teeth sank into his lower lip and he nodded. "That's why I want to find out who killed him and bring them to justice. All of them."

Her anger cooled as she realized she had no right to it. Agent Campbell was only doing his job, and not just because it was his job but because he'd cared about Sarge. And if she were him, she might have suspected her, too. She had been at the scene of two robberies.

She reached across the console and touched his hand. But it tensed beneath hers, tightening around the steering wheel. "I'm sorry," she said. "I understand that you have to question me. I just wish I could be more help for your investigation. I really don't have any idea who the robbers are."

He tugged his hand from beneath hers and reached

for the shifter, putting the car in Park after pulling into a space in the parking lot of her apartment complex.

She breathed a soft sigh of relief. He hadn't arrested her after all. He had actually brought her home. But she wasn't foolish enough to think that he no longer suspected her of being involved.

WAS HE BEING a fool? Blaine silently asked himself. Probably.

He should have taken her down to the Bureau or a local police department for questioning. But she was already trembling with exhaustion and dark circles rimmed her dark eyes. He wasn't heartless, but he hoped she wasn't playing him.

Maggie Jenkins had a sincerity and vulnerability that made him want to believe her and to believe that she was just an innocent victim.

Like Sarge...

He flinched over the loss of his friend. Instead of dealing with that death, he'd been busy trying to prevent another—to make sure that Maggie Jenkins stayed safe. He'd believed that was what Sarge had wanted. But what if his old friend had been trying to tell him something else about the assistant bank manager?

That she wasn't just involved in the robberies but maybe that she'd plotted them?

Her fingers trembled as she fumbled with the seat belt. Was she exhausted or was she nervous that he was questioning her? Or nervous that he'd brought her here?

He turned off the car, opened his door and hurried around the car to open hers. She was still having trouble with the seat belt, so he reached across her, brushed her fingers aside and undid the clasp. But now he was too close to her, too close to the curly hair that tumbled

around her shoulders, to the big brown eyes staring up
at him—to the full breasts that pushed against the thin
material of her blouse. He'd never considered a pregnant
woman sexy...until now. Until Maggie Jenkins...

Something shifted beneath his arm, which was pressed
to her belly, as if her baby was kicking him for the thoughts
he was entertaining. He jerked back and stepped away
from the car. She slid her legs out first. Since she'd lost her
shoe earlier, she wore slippers from the hospital. But she
didn't need to wear heels for her legs to look long and sexy.

Remembering how his sisters had struggled to get out
of cars while they were pregnant, he reached out to help
her. She clutched his hand but barely applied any pressure to pull herself up. And then she was standing right
in front of him, so close that her breasts nearly brushed
against his chest.

She tugged her hand free of his, and a bright pink
color flushed her face. "I—I don't have my purse," she
said. "I don't have my keys to get inside."

"You live alone?"

"Now I do," she replied. "But I can get an extra key
from my super." She glanced up to the darkening sky.
"If he's still awake..."

"You don't live with the baby's father anymore?" He
told himself he was asking only because of the case, but
he really wanted to know for himself.

She shook her head. "I never did..." And there was
something in her voice and her expressive eyes...an odd
combination of guilt and grief.

Blaine wanted to ask more questions but Maggie was
walking away from him. His skin chilled. It could have
been because of the cool wind that was kicking up as
night began to fall. It could have been because he had

an odd sense of foreboding—the same sense he'd had as he'd driven up to the bank during a robbery in progress.

He glanced around the parking lot. The complex was big—an L-shaped, four-story redbrick building, so there were a lot of vehicles parked in the lot. Quite a few of them were vans. Could one of them have been from the hospital? Could the robbers have followed them here?

He hurried and closed the distance between them, keeping his body between hers and the exposure to the parking lot. His hand was also on his holster, ready to pull his weapon should he need it.

Maggie rapped her knuckles hard against the door of a first-floor apartment. "My super's a little hard of hearing," she explained.

It took a couple more knocks before the door opened. A gray-haired man grinned at her. "Hey, Miss Maggie, what can I help you with?"

"Hi, Mr. Simmons. I left my purse at work," she said but spared him the details of why. "I'm so forgetful these days." She'd actually had other matters on her mind, but again she didn't share those with the older man. "So I need the extra key to my apartment, please."

His gray-haired head bobbed in a quick nod. "Of course I'll get that for you. Who's your friend?" His cloudy blue eyes narrowed as he studied Blaine. Apparently Blaine wasn't the only one in whom Maggie brought out protectiveness.

"Blaine Campbell. He's an old friend," she said, easily uttering the lie.

What else had she lied about?

The older man nodded again, accepting her explanation. "I'll be right back with the key."

After he disappeared, she turned toward Blaine and explained. "I didn't want to worry him. He knows the bank I worked at in Sturgis was robbed, so I told him I left the banking business."

"What does he think you do now?" he wondered.

"He thinks I work in an insurance office," she said, "which isn't really a lie since the bank does offer insurance policies."

Keys jangled as the old man returned to the doorway. "Have you checked on that renter's policy for me yet, Maggie?" he asked.

"Yes," she replied. "I'll bring that quote home tomorrow." She held out her hand for the key, but the gray-haired janitor glanced at Blaine again.

"You're an old friend of hers?" he asked with curiosity instead of doubt.

Blaine just nodded.

"Then you must've known her Andy?"

Andy? Was that the father of her baby? Blaine just nodded again.

"Thought you looked like you might've been a marine, too," the old guy said with another bob of his head.

"I was, sir," Blaine replied, and the admission reminded him of the man who had made him a marine. Sarge... "I served two tours."

"That's how you knew Sarge," Maggie said, softly enough that the older man probably didn't even hear her. "He was your drill sergeant?"

Blaine nodded. As a drill instructor, Sarge had been tough but fair. And he'd been a good and loyal friend.

"Glad you made it home, boy," Mr. Simmons said and reached out to pat Blaine's shoulder. "Too bad her fiancé didn't..."

"Andy," Blaine murmured, and the older man nodded again. Shocked and full of sympathy for her, Blaine turned toward Maggie. Earlier she'd told him that she was single, but she hadn't told him why. She hadn't said that her fiancé died before they could marry.

Her lashes fluttered furiously as she fought back tears over the loss of her baby's father. The hand she held out for the key began to tremble slightly. "Thank you for letting me use your spare, Mr. Simmons."

Finally the old man handed over the key she'd been waiting for. The second she closed her fingers around it, she rushed off toward the other end of the complex.

With a nod at the older man, Blaine hurried after her, careful to keep looking around to make sure nobody had followed them—the way someone must have followed the ambulance to the hospital.

But why?

If Maggie really had no idea who the robbers were, why had they wanted to kidnap her so desperately that they hadn't tried just once but twice?

Blaine stopped at the door where Maggie had stopped, her hand with the key outstretched toward the lock. She gasped. Hearing the fear in her voice, Blaine reached for his gun and pulled it from the holster.

Then he closed his free hand around Maggie's shoulder. She tensed and gasped again. Peering around her, he saw what she had—that the door to her apartment stood ajar. Since Maggie had said she lived alone now, someone must have broken in.

A thud emanated from the crack in the door. Whoever had broken in was still there. Waiting for Maggie...

Chapter Six

Like a rowboat riding on high waves, Maggie's stomach pitched as fear and nerves overwhelmed her. It was bad enough that the zombie robbers had tracked her down at the new bank branch where she worked and at the hospital where she'd been treated after the robbery. But had they now found out where she lived?

"Someone's inside," she whispered in horror.

But Blaine Campbell had already figured that out since he held his gun, the barrel pointing toward that crack in the door. He stood between her and her apartment. Between her and danger. "Go back to Mr. Simmons's apartment," he told her. "And stay there until I come for you."

She would have asked where he was going. But she knew. He had already walked into one robbery in progress today. So why wouldn't he walk into another?

Because he could get killed. Her hand automatically reached out with the impulse to hold him back—to protect him. But he was already pushing open the door a little farther and turning sideways as if to squeeze through. He turned back to her, his green gaze intense. "Go back to Mr. Simmons and call the police."

"Call them now," she urged him. "Don't go in there alone." As he had earlier…

He'd been lucky that the robbers hadn't killed him. If they hadn't been intent on getting away, they may have killed him just the way they had killed poor Sarge. If they'd kept shooting at him, they would have hit him where the vest wouldn't have protected him.

Dismissing her concern, he replied, "I'll be fine."

That was probably what Sarge had thought, too, when he showed up for work that morning. That he would be fine. But he hadn't. And she worried that neither would Agent Campbell.

"I'll be fine as long as you get out of here," he continued. "Now."

She had noticed and admired his commanding presence earlier. Now that it was directed at her, she resented it a bit. And she resented even more that she hurried to obey his command, turning away to head back to Mr. Simmons's apartment.

The minute the nearly deaf super let her inside, she would call the police. But they wouldn't arrive in time to help Agent Campbell. He was already stepping inside her apartment, already facing down danger.

Alone.

As Maggie lifted her hand to knock on the super's door, she heard the scream. It was high-pitched and full of fear.

THE WOMAN'S SCREAM caught Blaine off guard. He'd expected a masked robber. Or at least an armed threat. Instead he walked inside to find a woman—dressed like Maggie in a dark suit—rifling through the drawers of the dresser in what must have been Maggie's bedroom. Instead of being a peaceful oasis, it was full of color—oranges and greens and yellows. It was lively and vibrant, like her personality, except for those times when she'd been too scared to speak. It was also messy, but that might have been because of this woman rifling through Maggie's things.

"Who are you?" he asked, even though the blond-haired woman looked vaguely familiar. Where had he seen her before? The security footage from the hospital?

Could it have been a woman who had tried to abduct Maggie earlier? He doubted that a woman could have hurled the locker room bench with enough force to knock him down, but maybe that was just his ego talking. At the bank there had been one robber smaller than the others. He hadn't given it any thought then, because it could have been a short man. But it could have been a woman.

She just stared at him—her eyes wide with fear and guilt. She didn't hold a gun this time, though. Instead she held a velvet jewelry case in her hand.

"Who are you?" he repeated.

"It's Susan Iverson," another woman answered for her.

Wearing those damn slippers had made Maggie's footsteps silent—so silent that she would have been able to get the jump on him had she been one of the robbers. Hell, he had only her word that she wasn't one of them.

"Susan works at the bank, too. She's a teller," Maggie said, explaining how she knew the woman. "What are you doing here?"

"You left your purse at the bank," Susan replied. "I was bringing it back for you."

"And going through my stuff?"

Maggie was asking the questions he should have been asking. But her sudden nearness had distracted him—not so much that he had lowered the gun, though. He kept it trained on the obvious intruder.

"You used Ms. Jenkins's key to let yourself inside her

apartment?" he asked now. "That's still breaking and entering, you know."

"I used to live with her," Susan replied. She stared up at Blaine through her lashes, as if trying to flirt with him. "You're the FBI agent who rescued us this afternoon from those awful robbers."

"Yes, and you haven't answered the question." She hadn't answered any of the questions—neither had she dropped that little jewelry box.

He'd thought the robbers must have had an inside man. And maybe that thought had been right. Thinking Maggie was their accomplice was what had been wrong.

"You don't live with me anymore," Maggie said. "So you had no right to let yourself into my place." Her voice, usually so soft and sweet, was now sharp with anger and dislike.

"I brought your purse to you," Susan said again, as if she'd been doing Maggie a favor.

"You could have left it with the super," Blaine pointed out, "instead of letting yourself inside. What are you doing here, Ms. Iverson?"

At the moment she was trying to flirt with him—as if that could distract him from what she'd done now and what she might have done earlier. He'd never let a pretty face distract him...before Maggie.

The blonde smiled. "I was searching for clues," she said. "This is the second bank Maggie's worked at that's been robbed. Don't you think that's suspicious, Agent Campbell?"

A hiss accompanied the quick release of Maggie's breath—as if she'd been punched in the stomach. Maybe the baby had kicked her. Or maybe this woman casting suspicions her way had shocked her.

He had come up with suspicions about Maggie on his

own, but he wasn't about to admit it to this woman. At the moment she had become the better suspect. "I think your behavior is questionable right now, Ms. Iverson."

"You caught me—" she fluttered her lashes again "—playing amateur sleuth. I was only trying to help the bank recover the money that was stolen."

He wasn't charmed in the least by her coy attitude. "And you think hundreds of thousands of dollars are in that small jewelry case?"

She glanced down at it, as if just realizing it was in her hand. And she shook her head. Blond hair skimmed along her jaw with the movement. "I—I just found it as I was looking for the money."

Or was that what she'd been looking for? With the hand not holding his gun, he reached for the jewelry case. She held it tightly, but he tugged it from her grasping fingers. He popped open the case and a big square diamond glistened in the dim light of the nearly dark apartment.

Maggie reached out and snapped the case shut, as if she couldn't bear to look at the ring.

"Your engagement ring?" he asked her.

Her beautiful face tense, she nodded.

"I'm sorry," he said. It must have been hard for her to see the ring her dead fiancé had given her—especially after all she'd been through that day.

"Sorry?" the other woman asked with a disparaging snort. "She never even wore that ring. She probably wouldn't have noticed it missing…"

"So you did intend to steal it?" Blaine asked. He needed to grab his phone and call in this attempted robbery, but when he tried to hand the ring case over to Maggie, she drew back as if she couldn't touch it, either. So he shoved it into his pants pocket to reach for his cell. "I'm going to call the local authorities to book you, Ms. Iverson."

"No," Maggie said, reaching out now to grab his arm and stop him from calling. "I don't want to press charges."

"Why not?" he asked. He was furious with this woman, and he wasn't the one she'd been trying to rob.

Maggie just shook her head, and the blonde breathed a sigh of relief.

But Blaine ignored them both. "This needs to be reported and Ms. Iverson needs to be questioned about her involvement in the robberies."

"What involvement?" the woman asked, her already high voice squeaking with outrage. "I have no involvement."

"I'm not so sure about that…" She could have taken advantage of Maggie leaving her purse behind to try to steal the ring. Or she could have been here waiting for Maggie—to abduct her for the others.

"You think I was stealing the ring," the woman said. "Why would I need to pawn that for money if I was helping rob banks for millions of dollars?"

It wasn't quite millions. Not yet. But he worried that it would be if the robbers weren't stopped. And he worried that more people would die. The robbers had killed once, so it would be easier for them to kill again.

Was that what they'd intended to do with Maggie? Kill her? Why? To keep her quiet? And if they needed to keep her quiet, she had something to say—something she hadn't shared with him yet.

But then, there was a lot she hadn't shared with him. Maybe Susan Iverson wasn't the only one who needed to be brought in for questioning…

MAGGIE WAS SO exhausted that all she wanted to do was put on her comfy pajamas, crawl into her bed and sleep for days. But she was still wearing the skirt and blouse from her suit. And this wasn't her bed. It wasn't soft and comfortable. It was hard and cold—kind of like she was beginning to believe Agent Blaine Campbell might be.

Despite her protest, he'd had Susan arrested for breaking and entering, and attempted theft. He should have just let her take the ring.

Susan was right that Maggie had never worn it. She couldn't even look at it without remembering what Andy had sacrificed to buy her that ring. He'd bought it with the bonus for re-upping and volunteering for that last deployment—the one that had taken his life.

And she had never wanted the ring. She should have told him—should have made it clear that she didn't love him the way he had deserved to be loved. Andy had been a wonderful man, and he'd been taken too soon.

Like Sarge.

Could Susan have been involved in the robbery that had claimed his life? If she was, Maggie was certain that Agent Campbell would find out. With just a look he made Maggie want to confess all. But she had nothing to confess.

He didn't look as though he believed her, though. Was he cynical because of his FBI job and all he'd seen on it? Or was being a marine the reason he didn't trust easily?

Of course he had no reason to trust Maggie. He didn't know her.

If he knew her, he would have just let her stay in her apartment. But he'd insisted that she would be in danger in her own home. Susan knew she lived there, and if she were involved with the robberies, some of the others might try to kidnap her again—as they had at the hospital. So he'd had her brought here—to some sort of "safe" house.

But even with an officer standing outside the motel room door, Maggie didn't feel safe.

She had felt safe only with Agent Campbell. But he'd had Maggie brought here, and he'd gone down to the local police station with Susan.

Maggie was surprised that he hadn't taken her to the station, too. She knew he considered her every bit as much a suspect in the robberies as he did Susan. So maybe that officer wasn't posted outside the door for her protection. Maybe he was posted outside the door to keep her inside—to keep her from escaping.

But where would Maggie go?

She had already tried to escape once—when she'd moved from Sturgis to the Chicago suburb where she lived now. But the robbers had followed her.

Was it only the coincidence she wanted to believe it was? After all, the bank she'd worked at before and the one she worked at now weren't the only ones that had been robbed.

But that danger wasn't the only thing Maggie hadn't been able to leave in her past. When she'd let Susan stay with her, the woman had pried into her life. She'd learned about Andy. That was how Mr. Simmons had heard Maggie's sad story. Susan had used it when she'd been late with her part of the rent.

So Maggie hadn't been able to escape her guilt and loss, either. It had followed her, or maybe she was carrying it with her. She clasped her hands over the baby. She didn't want to escape him or her, though. She wanted to protect her baby—the way she hadn't been able to protect Andy. She'd thought that she was saving him from pain by keeping the truth of her feelings from him.

Maybe there was no escape from her past. But what about the danger? Was she really safe here?

Moments later she had her answer as gunfire erupted outside the motel room. She wasn't safe. The robbers had come for her again.

And this time Agent Campbell wouldn't arrive in time to save her...

Chapter Seven

In the dark Blaine fumbled around the top of the door-jamb for the key his friend had left for him. "I found it," he told Ash through the cell phone pressed to his ear. "I can't believe it's still here."

If he'd left a key outside his apartment in Detroit, it wouldn't have been there long; neither would any of the stuff in his apartment. He wouldn't have thought a Chicago suburb would be much safer—especially after he'd found an intruder in Maggie Jenkins's apartment.

Of course, that intruder had been someone she knew. Apparently she hadn't known her that well, though, if she'd ever trusted the treacherous woman. Not only had Susan tried to steal Maggie's engagement ring, but when Blaine searched her purse, he found that she'd helped herself to Maggie's credit and debit cards, as well.

Blaine blindly slid the key into the lock and quietly opened the door. Ignoring Ash's voice in his ear, he listened carefully for any sounds within the small bungalow. It was the only dark house on the street; that was how Ash had told him to find it.

At this hour everyone else was home—probably watching TV after dinner. What was Maggie Jenkins doing right now?

Eating?

Sleeping?

She'd looked exhausted. Maybe he should have insisted that she stay at the hospital for observation. But then, she hadn't been safe there, either.

"I told the neighbors to expect a tall blond guy to show up at my door within the next couple of days," Ash said.

This was the kind of neighborhood where people watched out their windows, aware of their surroundings and strangers. Because of Ash's warning, they gave Blaine only a cursory glance before their curtains and blinds snapped back into place and they returned to their television shows.

Blaine pushed open the door to a dark and empty house. "Thanks for giving them the heads-up," he said. "And thanks for letting me crash here."

Ash Stryker was also an FBI special agent but with the antiterrorism division, so he traveled more than Blaine did. Right now he was in DC or New York; Blaine couldn't remember which city. Hell, maybe it was neither. Since he specialized in homegrown terrorism, he could have been off in the woods somewhere. Blaine knew better than to ask. Ash was rarely at liberty to say.

"Thanks for calling me about Sarge," his friend replied, his voice gruff with emotion.

Blaine stopped in midreach for the light switch. While he dealt with his emotions over losing Sarge, he would rather stay in the dark, but he hadn't wanted to leave Ash there. He'd had to tell him about their loss. He and Ash went back before the Bureau. They had been marines together, too.

"I'm sorry," Blaine said. "So damn sorry…"

If only he could have done something.

If only he could have stopped Sarge from stepping out from behind that damn pillar.

But Sarge had reacted instinctively to Maggie's scream and had come to her rescue. If the former military man had actually thought she'd been involved in the robberies, he probably wouldn't have tried so hard to save her. But maybe he still would have done it—out of loyalty to her dead fiancé. He suspected Sarge had been Andy's drill instructor, as well.

"I'm going to try to make it home for his funeral," Ash promised. "Let me know when it is."

"Sure thing," Blaine replied. He knew his friend hated going to funerals as much as he did because they had attended way too many. They'd had so many friends who hadn't made it home—like Maggie's fiancé. "I'll tell you as soon as I find out when the arrangements are."

"Thanks," Ash said. "And feel free to make yourself at home."

"I won't be here long enough," Blaine said. He was more determined than ever to catch these bank robbers. He flipped on the switch and an overhead light flickered on, illuminating the sparsely furnished living room.

"I'm not there much, either." Ash stated the obvious. "If my uncle hadn't left me the place, I would probably just rent an apartment or a hotel room for when I'm in the city."

Blaine had wondered why his friend owned a house. Ash was a confirmed bachelor. The only commitment he'd ever made was to their country and the Bureau. "Like me," Blaine murmured.

Ash chuckled. "Well, you have sisters you can crash with when you have the urge to feel domestic."

Blaine groaned as he thought of the noise and chaos of his sisters' households. Kids crying. Throwing toys. His sisters yelling at their husbands. "Staying with them and their families reminds me why I'm single."

But then he thought of Maggie Jenkins and the baby that had moved beneath his touch. Maggie, with her friendly chatter, would fit in well with his family. Hell, she would fit in better than he ever had.

"So I'm warning you," Ash said, "that the fridge and cupboards are probably bare. There are take-out menus in the cupboard drawer by the fridge, though."

Blaine didn't feel like eating. Ever since that bullet had struck Sarge's chest, he had felt sick. Maggie Jenkins hadn't made him feel any better. He'd had local authorities take her into protective custody at a nearby motel. She would be safe.

He didn't need to worry about her. But he was worried. Did the single mom-to-be have anyone she could trust? Even her former roommate had been trying to steal from her. After interrogating Susan Iverson, Blaine believed that was probably the woman's only crime. He didn't think she was smart enough to be able to hide it if she were involved in the bank robberies.

"It's not your fault," Ash assured him. "You know Sarge. He would have never backed down from a fight— not even when he was outgunned."

Blaine sighed. "I know, especially since he was determined to protect the bank's assistant manager." He'd given up his life for hers and the baby's.

A large part of Ash's job was picking up subtext in recorded conversations. That was how he found threats to security. He easily picked up on Blaine's subtext, too. "Sounds like Sarge might not have been the only one wanting to protect this...*woman*?"

"Yes," Blaine admitted. "She's female. She's also young and pregnant." Too young to have already lost her fiancé, her baby's father...

"Married?" Ash inquired.

"No, her fiancé died in Afghanistan." And she must miss him so much that she couldn't even bear to look at the engagement ring he had given her. Blaine patted his pocket, but the ring was gone. He'd handed it over to the local authorities as evidence in Susan Iverson's attempted robbery—along with Maggie's credit and debit cards. He would make sure that Maggie got back the cards and the ring.

But he couldn't bring back what she probably wanted most. Her fiancé…

While Blaine had dated over the years, he'd gotten over the breakups easily enough to know that he had never been in love. He couldn't relate to Maggie's pain, losing the man with whom she'd intended to spend the rest of her life. It had been hard enough losing the friends he'd lost over the years and now losing Sarge.

"Was her fiancé one of Sarge's former drills?"

He sighed. "I think so." It would explain why, after retiring from the military, Sarge had taken a part-time job in a bank. Maybe he'd heard about Maggie getting robbed at the first bank, and he'd intended to protect her. Or maybe she had switched to the bank where Sarge was working because she'd obviously known him. Sarge had always stayed in touch with his former drills.

"Then the old man would have been happy he died saving her," Ash said.

Blaine hadn't expected his cynical friend to come up with such a romantic notion. He blinked hard as his eyes began to burn. "Yeah, he would have been…" He sighed. "But the threat isn't over for Maggie Jenkins. One of the robbers tried grabbing her from the ER where the paramedics took her after the robbery."

"You stopped him, though." Ash just assumed.

"This time."

"You'll keep Maggie safe for Sarge."

Blaine wasn't so sure about that. He had that feeling again—that chill racing up and down his spine—that told him all was not well. The thought had no more than crossed his mind when his phone beeped with an incoming call.

"I have to go, Ash." He didn't waste time with good-byes, just clicked over the phone to take the next call. "Agent Campbell."

"Agent, this is Officer Montgomery," a man identified himself. He then continued, "We have a report of shots fired at the motel where we took the bank-robbery witness."

He cursed, and his stomach knotted with dread. The motel was nearby, but probably still too far for him to get there in time to save her.

MAGGIE STARED AT the locked bathroom door, waiting for somebody to kick it down or riddle it with bullets. But as she listened, an eerie silence had fallen where only moments before gunfire had deafened her.

She'd wanted to press her hands over her ears and hide under the covers in the dark motel room. But this wasn't a nightmare from which she could hide. So she had forced herself to jump out of the bed and run into the bathroom. Once in there she had locked the door and barricaded it shut by wedging the vanity chair beneath the knob. As a barricade, it was flimsy; it wouldn't take someone much to kick open the door and drag her out.

But she wasn't worried just about herself or about her baby. Had the officer who'd been stationed outside the door of her room been hurt or worse? Her stomach lurched with dread because she suspected the worst. If he was fine, wouldn't he have checked on her? Wouldn't he have at least knocked on the bathroom door and assured her it was safe to come out?

But Maggie wasn't even safe in a safe house.

Blaine Campbell was right. Even though she had no idea what it was, she must have seen or heard *something* that could identify at least one of the robbers. Why else would they so desperately want her dead?

Unable to stare at the door any longer, she squeezed her eyes shut. And she prayed. She prayed for that young officer who had only been doing his job. Like Sarge, trying to protect her.

And she prayed for her baby. Her hands trembled as she splayed them across her belly. Nothing shifted or kicked beneath her palms. For once the child slept—blissfully unaware of the danger he and his mother faced.

Was this all Maggie's fault?

Maybe karma didn't think she deserved the baby because she hadn't loved the baby's father the way she should have. Andy had been such a sweet guy; he hadn't deserved to die. And neither did his baby.

Maggie had to keep him or her safe. But there was no window in the bathroom, no way of escaping except through the door she had barricaded. But the shooting had been out front. Whoever had been shooting at the young police officer could already be inside the motel room, just waiting for her to leave the bathroom.

But the gruesomely masked gunman hadn't waited for her to leave the hospital. He had walked right into the emergency department and dragged her from her bed.

If one of those masked gunmen were inside the motel room, he wouldn't wait long for her to come out. He would break down the door to get to her.

To kill her? What else could they want with her?

She had no money to offer them. But after all the

banks they had robbed, they shouldn't need any more money. Some people, however, never thought they had enough. So maybe they wanted to keep robbing banks and for some reason thought she had the knowledge to stop them…

So they wanted to stop her from talking. They wanted to kill her.

As if her fearful thoughts had conjured up one of the men, the door rattled as someone tried to turn the knob. The chair legs squeaked against the vinyl floor, moving as someone wrenched harder on the knob—determined to get to her.

Could she convince them that she knew nothing? That she had no idea who they were?

It was the only chance she had. But she would be able to pull it off only if they still wore the masks. What if they didn't? Then she couldn't look at them—because they would kill her for sure.

The door rattled harder—metal hinges creaking, wood cracking. In case they came in firing, she climbed into the bathtub. She put her face down on her knees and wrapped her arms around the back of her head. Her stance wouldn't protect her or the baby from bullets. But she had no other way to protect herself…

The chair toppled over against the sink, and the door flew open with such force that the wood cracked against the side of the bathtub. Someone must have kicked it in.

But she didn't dare look up. She didn't want to be able to identify any of the robbers. She wanted the danger to end. She actually wanted Blaine Campbell and his protection. But he was too far away to protect her.

"Please leave me alone," she begged. "You don't have to hurt me. I don't know anything about the robberies. And I don't care…"

All she cared about was her baby. She actually hadn't been thrilled when she'd found out she was pregnant. But then Andy had died and she'd been relieved that she hadn't lost him completely.

But now she wasn't just going to lose that last piece of Andy—she was going to lose her own life, too.

Chapter Eight

Guilt had Blaine's shoulder slumping slightly. Or maybe he'd hurt it when he had broken down the bathroom door. "Maggie, it's me," he said.

But she kept her arms locked around her head, her body trembling inside the bathtub. Curled up the way she was, she looked so small—so fragile—so frightened.

He hadn't dared to say who he was as he broke down the door…because he hadn't known what he would find inside. Maggie might not have been alone. One of the gunmen might have gotten to her and barricaded them both inside the bathroom when he'd arrived. Or it might have only been one of the gunmen inside the bathroom and Maggie might have already been gone.

Blaine hadn't arrived quite in time. The officer outside the door had been shot. Maybe mortally…

Sirens wailed outside the motel as more emergency vehicles careened into the lot. Hopefully an ambulance was among them—with help for the young cop and for Maggie.

Maybe she needed medical attention, too. Had any of the shots fired at the officer struck her? Blaine looked into the tub again, but he noticed no blood on the white porcelain—only Maggie's dark curls spread across the cold surface.

"Maggie!" He reached out for her.

But she swung her hands then, striking out at him. "Leave me alone! Leave me alone!"

He caught her wrists and then lifted her wriggling body from the tub and into his arms. "Maggie! It's me— it's Blaine!"

Finally she looked up, her dark eyes wide as she stared at him in wonder. "Blaine!" Then she threw her arms around his neck and clung to him.

And his guilt increased. He never should have left her to the protection of anyone else. The young officer had been shot, and Maggie might have been taken if he hadn't gotten there in time. The wounded officer had held off the gunmen until Blaine had arrived.

Then Blaine had fired on them, too. He didn't think that he'd hit any of them, though. And tires had squealed as a van had sped out of the parking lot.

For a long, horrible moment he'd thought that Maggie might have been in that van. That he had been too late to save her. Then he had found the bathroom door locked inside the room, and he'd hoped that she'd hidden away. But Blaine had been doing this job too long to be optimistic. So he had expected the worst—that one of the gunmen had been left behind and barricaded himself alone or, worse yet, inside the bathroom with Maggie.

In a ragged sigh of relief, her breath shuddered out against his throat. She had undoubtedly expected the worst when he'd broken open the door.

He wrapped his arms tightly around Maggie, holding her close. She trembled against him—as if she couldn't stop shaking. She was probably in shock.

"I'm sorry," he said.

But he had to pull away and leave her again—only because he had to make sure that help had arrived for the young officer and for Maggie. He wanted a doctor to check her out again.

He wanted to make sure that she was all right.

How much fear could she and her baby handle?

There was only one way that Blaine would truly be able to protect her, the way Sarge had wanted and died trying to do. And that was to find out who was so determined to grab her or kill her.

Who were the bank robbers?

ONE OF THE paramedics assured Maggie and Agent Campbell that she was fine. Apparently she couldn't die from fear.

What about embarrassment?

She had embarrassed herself when she cried out his name and clung to him. She had acted like a girlfriend when he considered her a robbery suspect.

Or had he changed his mind about that?

Then he took her to his home—although *home* was stretching it. The bungalow obviously belonged to a single man. There were no pictures on the walls. No knickknacks on the built-in shelves. Not even a book or a magazine.

The living room held a couch and a chair while the dining room contained a desk instead of a table. The table was in the kitchen, but it had only two chairs at it. There was a bed in each of the two bedrooms.

Blaine showed her to one while taking the other for himself. Maybe she slept. Maggie wasn't sure. She drifted in and out, occasionally hearing Blaine's voice. She doubted he slept at all. He had been on his cell phone instead.

The house was quiet now. But Maggie knew he hadn't left because she smelled food. Bacon. And coffee. Her stomach grumbled, but she stayed in bed, not eager to face him. Her face heated even now, as she thought of how she'd acted.

Like a girlfriend…

But Blaine Campbell was just an FBI agent doing his job. He probably had a girlfriend somewhere, because a man that handsome was unlikely to be single. Unless Blaine's only commitment was his career…

She had to stop thinking of him as Blaine and remember that he was Special Agent Campbell. That was all he was and all he would ever be to her.

The baby kicked. Apparently they both wanted food. So she tossed back the covers and kicked her legs over the side of the bed. The T-shirt Blaine had loaned her as a nightgown had ridden up, revealing her high-cut briefs. She reached to tug down the hem of the shirt just as someone cleared his throat.

"Sorry," Blaine said, as he had the night before when he'd peeled her off him.

She was the one who should be apologizing—for inconveniencing him as she had. For costing him a friend like Sarge. For making his job harder. But for once she, who usually couldn't stop talking, couldn't find words to express herself and her gratefulness for his saving her over and over again.

"I was just coming up to see if you were awake," he said. "I had some groceries delivered and made breakfast."

The man could cook? He really was perfect.

But perfect wasn't for Maggie—not with the mess her life had become. She pulled the T-shirt down, but it was still short enough that it left her legs bare. And, in her mind, Blaine's gaze skimmed down her legs like a caress.

But that could only be in her mind—her imagination.

The FBI agent couldn't really be interested in her. Not for anything but information…

He proved that a short while later when he picked her empty plate up from the table and started asking questions. "You're sure that you didn't recognize anyone from the robberies?"

"I'm sure," she said. "I only recognized those horrible masks from the robbery at the Sturgis branch where I used to work." She shuddered as she thought of the grotesque masks. They could have come right from that R-rated zombie movie she'd gone to so long ago. "With the masks and the trench coats, I couldn't see any facial features or even body types of the robbers."

"You're not protecting anyone?"

She shook her head. But her hands automatically covered her belly. The baby had stopped moving. Maybe the food had satiated him. The cheesy scrambled eggs, crisp bacon and wheat toast had been delicious—so delicious that Maggie had probably eaten more than she should have.

But then, she could barely remember the last time she'd eaten. Some crackers at the hospital? Before that a breakfast she'd made herself—lumpy oatmeal with too much brown sugar. She would have to learn to be a better cook for the baby. If she lived long enough to cook for him…

"I want to protect my baby," she said. But she feared that she was going to fail, just as she had failed Andy. "That's the only person I'm protecting. So if I knew anything about the robbers, I would tell you."

"You haven't noticed anyone hanging around the bank, casing the place?" he asked.

She shook her head again. "I don't know what casing a place looks like. So I can't say that someone hasn't done

it." Obviously they had or they wouldn't have pulled off
the robbery so easily—until Blaine had arrived. If only
he could have saved Sarge…

Blaine hadn't eaten nearly as much as she had. Most
of his food was on his plate yet, forgotten, as he asked
his questions. "Nobody came around both of the banks?"

Once again, she shook her head. "The branches are far
enough away that they had different customers. I knew
most of the clients from Sturgis since I'd worked at that
branch since I graduated, but I'm just getting to know the
people at this branch." Should she bother? Or should she
move on again to another branch, another city?

How would she work there without remembering those
robbers bursting in? That was why she'd left Sturgis. Because of the memories. But there were worse ones here;
there was Sarge getting shot and dying.

"What about workers?" Blaine asked. "Did Susan
work at both branches, too?"

"No," she said. "I'm the only one who worked at both
branches." Which was why he had suspected she was involved, and she couldn't blame him for his suspicions.
"But I really have nothing to do with the robberies."

He didn't look at her the way he had before, as if he
doubted her.

Hope fluttered in her chest like her baby fluttered in
her belly, waking up from his or her short nap. "Do you
believe me?" she asked.

He uttered a heavy sigh of resignation. "I believe that
you're not consciously involved."

She should have been happy that he didn't think she
was a criminal mastermind, but his comment dented her
pride. He clearly thought she was an idiot instead. "I'm
not *unconsciously* involved, either."

"You haven't told anyone about your job?" he asked.

"Most people know that I work at a bank," she said, "except for Mr. Simmons."

"Because you don't want to worry him," he said with a slight smile, as if amused or moved.

She sighed. "That was all for nothing after you called the cops on Susan. He probably knows now. But that's all anyone knows about me—that I work there."

"You haven't told anyone any details that might make it easier for them to hold up the bank," he persisted, "to know which days you'd have the most cash on hand?"

"No," she replied, pride stinging at how stupid he thought her. He wasn't the only one who'd thought that. Because she talked a lot, people sometimes thought she was flighty. But her grades in school and college had proved them all wrong. She talked a lot because she really didn't like silence. It made her uncomfortable, so she generally tended to fill it with chatter.

"You don't talk to your family about your job?" he asked skeptically. "You wouldn't share any details with them?"

So now he thought her family members were criminal masterminds? She corrected that misassumption. "For his job, my dad and mom moved to Hong Kong a couple of years ago."

And since Andy's death, all they talked about was the weather—asking about hers, telling about theirs. Their conversations didn't get any deeper; they were probably afraid that they might make her cry if they brought up something that would remind her of Andy. Or maybe it would make them cry because they'd loved him like a son.

"You don't have any brothers or sisters?" he asked.

"No." And because she was sick of being the only one

answering questions, she started asking some of her own. "What about you?"

"I have three older sisters," he replied, and his lips curved into a slight smile as his green eyes crinkled a little at the corners.

Growing up, she had wanted sisters. But her father had been busy with his career, and her mom hadn't wanted to raise more than one child alone. Maggie would really be raising her baby alone.

She shook off the self-pity before she could wallow and asked, "Any brothers?"

"Just in arms," he replied.

Fellow marines. Andy had called them brothers, too. She sighed.

"Do you have any *friends* that you're really close to?" he asked. "Anyone that you would talk to without realizing that you might have let some information slip?"

He really thought she was an idiot. But maybe she had been—because she had told someone more than she should have.

Since he watched her closely, he must have caught her reaction as her realization dawned. "There is someone," he concluded. "Who?"

"It doesn't make a difference now," she said.

"Who is it?" he asked, his voice sharp as if he thought she was protecting someone.

"Andy," she said. "I told Andy everything…" Since they were kids, he had been her best friend, her confidant.

His blond head bobbed in a sharp nod. "Of course…"

But then she realized that she'd lied to the agent. She hadn't told Andy everything, or she would have told him the truth—that she didn't love him as anything more than her best friend. Maybe she'd told him so much about the bank because, as with her parents just discussing the weather, she had preferred to talk to Andy about her job than about her feelings or their future. She hadn't seen one for them, but not because she'd thought he was going to die.

"But Andy's gone," she said. "So there's no way he could have had anything to do with the bank robberies."

"Can I ask...how did he die?"

For once she was short with her words. "He drove a supply truck. An IED took out the whole convoy."

He flinched. "I'm sorry."

She nodded. It was her automatic reaction to everyone's condolences. Condolences she didn't feel she really deserved, just the way she felt she hadn't deserved Andy.

"Would Andy have told anyone what you told him?" Blaine asked.

"Why?" While he had listened to her, Andy really hadn't cared about her job. He'd been proud that she'd gone to college, that she'd gotten her degree in finance, but he'd thought that she would quit working once they got married and started having kids.

Andy really hadn't known her at all. Or he would have guessed that, while she loved him, she wasn't in love with him. So if Andy hadn't known her that well, maybe she hadn't known him, either.

"I can think of hundreds of thousands of reasons why he might have told someone," Blaine replied.

Maggie defended her friend. "Andy didn't care about money."

"But that was quite a ring he bought you..."

He hadn't just paid for that ring with money; he'd paid for it with his life, too. "He used his bonus—for re-upping and for his last deployment..."

Blaine nodded as if she'd answered another question—

one that he hadn't actually asked. "Maybe he didn't realize that he was revealing anything."

She hadn't realized that something she'd said could have led to those robberies, to Sarge's death. She hoped Blaine was wrong because she already had too much guilt to live with; she didn't need any more.

Chapter Nine

Maggie insisted on going to the bank, and Blaine agreed. The bank wasn't open for business, though. Not yet. Repairmen were working on replacing the broken windows and fixing the damaged walls and furniture. So Blaine took her around the back, through the security door that the robbers had dragged her out.

That was hard enough—watching her face drain of color as she relived those moments. She probably hadn't thought she was going to get away from the robbers. And for a few moments Blaine hadn't thought he was going to get her away from them—then or later at the hospital or the motel.

He relived all those moments and found his arm coming around her thin shoulders. "Maybe this was a bad idea," he murmured.

"I need to go to my office," she said. "And make sure I didn't leave anything out yesterday."

"The manager closed up the bank yesterday," he assured her. "I'm sure he locked up whatever paperwork you might have had out."

He did not want her going to her office. Since her walls were glass, it had also been damaged from the gunfire. And in the lobby was the outline where Sarge's body had been. She didn't need to see that, and neither did he.

.

Maggie shook her head. "No, Mr. Hardy wouldn't have done it himself. He probably let Susan do it and that's how she got hold of my purse."

Blaine hadn't been that impressed with the manager—especially when the guy had been firing questions at her while the paramedics were trying to assess her condition. It was obvious that most of the day-to-day administration had fallen on Maggie's slim shoulders. "She got your purse, your keys and your credit cards."

She sighed. "I should cancel my credit cards."

"She already used a couple of them," he said. While Maggie had been at the hospital, the greedy woman had used her cards. "Why did you ever have her as your roommate?"

Maggie shrugged hard enough to dislodge his arm and stepped away from his side. Maybe he had offended her by implying that she wasn't the greatest judge of character. "She was really nice to me when I first started working here," she said in defense of their relationship, "so I agreed to let her move in when her boyfriend kicked her out and she had nobody else to stay with."

He wondered if that had been a ruse. Maybe he had underestimated Susan Iverson's intelligence. He would take another look at her. But first he wanted Maggie to look at something; that was why he had agreed to bring her down to the bank.

He had also wanted to get out of Ash's small house before he lost all objectivity where Maggie Jenkins was concerned. She was too damn beautiful for his peace of mind. He couldn't lose the image of her hair tangled from sleep, her body all soft and warm and sexy. When she'd tossed back the blankets and revealed her bare legs and the shapely curve of her hips, he had been tempted to crawl into bed with her.

She sighed again. "But I learned quickly why her boyfriend had kicked her out."

"The woman can't be trusted." Blaine wondered if this one could. He wanted to trust Maggie Jenkins; he wanted to believe she was every bit as sweet and innocent as she seemed.

But he couldn't rule out any possible suspects yet. And she was a possible one—even after the attempts on her life. Or maybe because of them. Her coconspirators could be trying to prevent her from giving them up.

He led Maggie to a back office, near the rear exit, where he had had the bank security footage set up across six small monitors. He pressed a remote and started it rolling.

"What is all this?" she asked.

"Security footage." Sarge's security footage. "I want you to watch it."

"All of it?" She sounded overwhelmed. The six monitors probably were a bit daunting.

Blaine was used to it, as he often watched days, sometimes weeks or even months, of security footage when he was investigating bank robberies. But this time while they watched the monitors, he saw only Maggie—her full breasts and belly pushing against his old T-shirt. Those long, bare legs...

How would they feel wrapped around him? How would she feel when he buried himself inside her?

He shook his head, shaking off the thoughts. *They* would never happen. She wasn't just pregnant with another man's child; she was still in love with that man. It didn't matter that Andy was dead. A love like theirs—where she had told him *everything*—was deep and enduring.

Blaine had never had anyone in his life to whom he'd told *everything*. He had learned at a young age that if he told his sisters anything they would tell *everyone*. So he'd been keeping his own counsel for a long time— which was good because he had no intention of sharing his thoughts about Maggie with anyone else. In fact, he wanted to forget all about them.

So he focused on the video screens playing out on the monitors in Sarge's office. It might have been hard to be there, if Sarge hadn't been like Blaine and Ash—too nomadic to personalize any space. It wasn't as if they would be there long enough to put down roots anyway. If Ash hadn't inherited that house in the Chicago burbs, he would have just had an apartment like Blaine had in Detroit—something devoid of decoration and sparsely furnished.

Days of security footage passed before his eyes in a blur—slow enough to pick out faces but fast enough that hours passed in minutes. His head began to pound— maybe more from his mostly sleepless night than from watching the footage.

If staring at those monitors had affected him, he worried how it was affecting Maggie. "Are you okay?" he asked her.

Maggie nodded. "I'm fine." But her fingers touched her temple and she closed her eyes.

"We can take a break," he offered.

"I don't understand why we're watching *these* videos," she said as she gestured at the screens. "All of this happened a week or more ago."

Had she expected him to show her the footage of the robbery? That would have been too much for her—to relive those terrifying moments, to relive Sarge getting killed…

He may have already told her. So much had happened

that he couldn't remember exactly, so he asked, "Do you know why I showed up when I did yesterday?"

"Because you're working those bank robberies."

That was what he'd told the state troopers in the alley. "Sarge called me," Blaine said. "He told me that he thought the bank was going to be hit."

She gasped in surprise. "He knew?"

"Yeah, he must have realized that someone was casing the place." And hopefully that someone had been picked up on the security footage.

She shrugged. "But *I* don't know how to tell who's casing the place."

"I do," he said. While he'd worked his way up in the Bureau through other divisions, he specialized in bank robberies now. To date, his record was perfect; he always caught the thieves.

Always…

And this time he had even more incentive than his record and his career. He had Sarge. And Maggie…

"So what am *I* looking for?" she asked.

"Someone you know."

She laughed as if he'd said something ridiculous. "I know a lot of these people."

He could tell. Even though she hadn't been at this branch that long, she often stepped out of her office to talk to bank clients, her face breathtakingly beautiful as she smiled welcomingly at them. They all smiled back, charmed by her friendly personality.

But he stopped the footage on one monitor as he noticed that one man smiled bigger than the others. And he hadn't left his greeting at a smile. He had gone in for a hug—a big one that had physically lifted Maggie off her feet. She hadn't looked happy, though; she had looked uncomfortable.

"Who's that?" he asked.

She stared at the screen, her eyes wide and face pale as if she'd seen a ghost. "I always forget how much he looks like Andy..."

"Who is he?"

She released a shaky breath. "Mark—that's Andy's older brother, Mark."

"Does he have accounts at the bank?"

She shook her head. "No, he just came by to see me. To check on me."

Blaine's senses tingled as he recognized a viable lead. "Did he use to come by the other branch you worked at?"

"Sometimes."

He nodded.

"It's not what you think," she assured him.

She had no idea what he was thinking. People rarely did. He wasn't even thinking of the case. He was thinking that the man wasn't just looking at her with concern or familial affection. He was looking at her with attraction. The way Blaine looked at her...

But in the footage she wasn't looking at the man at all. Like the ring, it was as if she couldn't bear to look at him. Because he looked so much like her dead fiancé?

He was a good-looking man. With their frequently inappropriate comments, his sisters would've gone on and on about his dark hair and light-colored eyes. And Andy had looked like that?

A weird emotion surged through Blaine—anger or resentment? Jealousy?

He was jealous of a dead man...

"WHAT AM I THINKING?" Blaine was asking her, his voice gruff with a challenge as if he doubted she could read him.

Few people probably could. The man was incredibly

guarded. But he'd let that guard down, briefly, to mourn the loss of his friend and former drill instructor. So Maggie felt as if she had found a tiny hole in his armor.

"You're thinking that Mark is involved in the robberies," she replied. "And that's ridiculous."

Blaine turned back to the monitor and studied the frozen frame of Mark lifting her off her feet. That muscle twitched in his cheek—almost as if it bothered him that another man was holding her.

But her thought was even more ridiculous than his thinking that Mark Doremire was a robber. Blaine Campbell was not jealous of another man touching her. Blaine had no interest in her beyond helping him figure out who the robbers were.

"Why is it ridiculous?" Blaine asked.

"Because he's Andy's brother."

A blond brow arched, as if that made Mark guiltier. Because of what she'd told Andy? If only she'd kept her mouth shut…

Maybe her mother had been right—she talked too much. Or, in this case, she'd written too much.

Once again, she defended her best friend. "Andy was the most honest person I've ever known."

Blaine didn't challenge her opinion of Andy. He just pointed out, "That doesn't mean that his brother is honest, too."

"I understand their personalities being different. But not their fundamental beliefs. They were raised by the same parents—raised the same way," she said. "How could they be that different?"

"You are obviously an only child." He laughed. "I have three sisters, and they are very different from each other."

"How?" she asked. She had always wished she'd had siblings. But her dad's career was demanding, and he hadn't been around that much to help her mother. So Mom had won the argument to have only one child.

He laughed again. "Sarah is a car salesperson—with that over-the-top bubbly personality. Erica is a librarian—quiet and introspective. And Buster…"

"Buster?" She'd thought he'd said they were all sisters.

"Becky is her real name," he explained. "She's in law enforcement, too. She's a county deputy. So my sisters are absolutely nothing alike."

"Maybe not personality-wise," she said. Mark and Andy hadn't been that much alike, either. Mark had liked to tease and joke around, and Andy had always been so sensitive and serious. "But morality and ethics…"

"Sarah sells cars," he repeated. "I'm not so sure about the ethics…"

She laughed now. From the twinkle in his green eyes, it was obvious how much he loved all of his sisters—even the car salesperson.

"Mark has been coming around *because* of his ethics," she said, "because he made a promise to Andy—the last time Andy left for a deployment—that he would take care of me if something happened to him."

That blond brow lifted again with a question and suspicion. "How is he taking care of you?"

If he was asking what she thought he was…

She shuddered in revulsion. "Not like *that*. Mark is like my brother, too. We all grew up together."

Blaine clicked the remote and unfroze Mark's image. Andy's brother kept smiling at her…before Susan walked up and started flirting with him. "What about with her?" he asked. "Is he brotherly with Susan Iverson?"

She hoped not. "Mark is married. He's not interested in Susan." But as she watched the footage, she wondered. "Maybe he's just a flirt…" Sometimes it felt as if he was flirting with her, which always made her extremely uncomfortable. Because she really thought of Mark as a big brother and only a big brother.

"I need to talk to Mark," Blaine said. "Where can I get hold of him?"

"I think I have his address somewhere in my office. He and his wife invited me to dinner before." But she had politely declined because it was so hard to see him. "I can call him…"

She would really prefer calling him to seeing him.

But Blaine shook his head. "I'll get his address from your office. Then I'll put you back into protective custody."

"Because that worked out so well last time?" she asked. "How is that young officer?" Before they had left the little bungalow for the bank, Blaine had called the hospital to check on him, but all he'd told her was that the young man had made it through surgery.

"He's still in critical condition," he said.

"Then just let me call Mark," she urged, her heart beating fast with panic at the thought of being separated from Blaine again. "You can talk to him—you'll know that he had nothing to do with the robberies."

But Blaine shook his head in refusal. "No, I have to see him face-to-face."

So he had to leave her again.

And every time he left, there was another attempt to grab her. One of these times the attempt was destined to be successful.

Would this be the time?

Chapter Ten

Every time Blaine left her alone or in someone else's protection, Maggie Jenkins was in danger. He didn't want to risk it again. It was better that she stayed with him. So she sat in the passenger seat of the FBI-issued SUV that had replaced his rental sedan as he drove to her almost brother-in-law's address.

But now was he the one putting her in danger?

He shouldn't have brought her along with him. But he couldn't risk a phone call that might have tipped off Mark Doremire to his suspicions. If the man was one of the robbers, he certainly had enough money to escape the country—to one where there was no extradition.

Hell, he was probably already gone.

But then, who kept trying to grab Maggie or kill her? And why? If she could identify them, wouldn't it be easier to escape now than to stick around to try to kill her?

"This trip is a waste of time," she remarked from the passenger's seat. "Mark won't be able to help you, either— just like I couldn't help you this morning at the bank."

She had helped him. He'd found a possible suspect. She just didn't want to see that her dead fiancé's brother could be a suspect.

"I watched all that footage and I didn't notice anyone *casing* the bank," she said, her soft voice husky with frustration. "I didn't notice anything out of the ordinary. And I didn't at the first bank that was robbed."

He should have brought up that footage, too. But she'd already admitted that Mark Doremire had been at that bank. Both banks had been robbed—it was a coincidence that was worth checking out.

But he should have checked it out alone. "You really shouldn't be along with me," he said regretfully.

"No," she agreed, even though it had been her comments that had talked him out of risking her safety to someone else's responsibility. "I don't want to see Mark. And I really don't want to see one of those zombie robbers again." She shuddered with revulsion. "Maybe I should go stay with my parents in Hong Kong."

His pulse leaped in reaction to her comment, to the thought of her going away where he couldn't protect her, where he couldn't see her. "You can't leave the country."

"Why?" she asked, her voice sharp with anger. "Am I still a suspect?"

He wasn't sure what she was. Entirely too distracting. Entirely too attractive...

He couldn't let her leave. "Right now you're a material witness."

"Some witness," she said disparagingly. "I can't help you at all. I didn't see anything on that footage. And during the robberies I only saw what everyone else saw— trench coats and zombie masks." She shuddered again at mention of the disguises.

She obviously hated those gruesome masks.

"You heard one of them speak," he reminded her.

She shrugged. "But I didn't recognize his voice."

So it hadn't been Mark Doremire who'd spoken. But it could have been someone he knew—a friend of his. "You might if you were to hear it again."

She sighed with resignation. "That's true. I doubt I'll forget him announcing the robbery the minute they walked into the bank."

Like the guns and disguises hadn't given away their intentions.

Announcing a robbery made them seem more like rookies than professionals. But then, they hadn't been robbing banks that long. Less than a year—barely half a year, actually. Blaine would catch them before they went any longer. If he had his way, the last bank they robbed would be the one at which Sarge had died.

"Which house is it?" he asked as he turned the black SUV onto the street on which Mark Doremire lived. The SUV would probably give away Blaine's identity, but he tucked his badge inside his shirt.

"I don't know," Maggie replied. "I haven't been here before." She leaned forward and peered at the numbers on the houses. "That one…"

This neighborhood wasn't like Ash's. Nobody looked out the windows. They probably looked the other way. The houses were in ill repair, with missing shingles and paint peeling off. If Mark had stolen any of the money, he hadn't spent it yet—at least not on his house.

"I'll stay in the car," she offered.

Blaine turned toward her. Her face was pale, as if she'd already seen a ghost. "I can't leave you in the car."

"Why not?"

"Someone could have followed us."

She glanced around fearfully. "Did someone?"

He doubted it; he had been too careful. "I don't know. But I don't want you out of my sight."

He didn't want her walking into the line of fire, either. So he handed her his cell phone. "Call him."

"But we're already here…"

If she tipped Mark off now and he ran, Blaine was close enough to catch him. He'd also radioed in his intentions to speak to a possible suspect. So other agents and the local authorities knew where he was and there was a deputy in the vicinity.

"Call him."

She sighed but looked down at the piece of paper that had Mark's address and cell phone. Then she punched in a number. "It didn't even ring. It went straight to his voice mail. Do you want— Oh, his voice mail is full." With another sigh, of relief, she hung up the phone.

Straight to voice mail? That wasn't a good sign— especially since the house looked deserted. Maybe he had already left. Just then an older car, with rust around the wheel wells and on the hood, pulled up across from them and parked at the curb in front of the house.

"That's his wife," Maggie said as a red-haired woman stepped from the car.

Nobody else was inside the vehicle, so seeing no threat to Maggie's safety, Blaine opened his door. "Mrs. Doremire."

She jumped as if startled. But then, in a neighborhood like this, it probably was strange for someone to call out her name. It was probably strange for anyone to even know her name. She slowly turned around and stared at him. "Yes?"

"Tammy," Maggie called out to her.

The woman peered around him and noticed Maggie inside the SUV. She smiled and waved. "Hi, there. Mark will be thrilled that you finally came over to visit."

"Is he here?" Blaine asked.

Tammy turned her attention back to him, and her brow furrowed with confusion. "I'm sorry…"

"Blaine." He introduced himself with his first name

only. If the press had mentioned him in any reports about the bank robbery, it would have been as Special Agent Campbell. "I'm a friend of Maggie's."

And, really, friendship was all he could expect from her—even though he wanted so much more. He wanted *her.*

"I'm sorry," Tammy Doremire said again, as she crossed the street to the SUV. "Mark isn't here right now."

"Where is he?"

She sighed. "He's at one of his folks'—probably his dad's."

"Dad's?" Maggie asked. "Mr. and Mrs. Doremire aren't together anymore?"

"They split up after Andy died," she said. "It was too much for them. So Mark keeps checking on them, like he checks on you, Maggie. He's trying so hard to take care of everybody since Andy's gone."

Maggie's voice cracked as she apologized now. "I'm sorry…"

It wasn't her fault that Andy had died. It was whoever had set the damn IED where the convoy would hit it. But Mark's wife didn't absolve her of guilt. She only shrugged.

"Sometimes he'll stay the night at his dad's," she said, "so you'll probably want to come back tomorrow."

Maggie nodded in agreement. But Blaine had other plans.

"It was nice meeting you, Mrs. Doremire," he said as he slid back behind the wheel.

She nodded, but her brow was furrowed again—as if she'd realized she hadn't really met him. He had only told her his first name.

"We'll come back tomorrow, then," he lied.

"Why?" Maggie asked after he'd closed his door. "You can tell Mark has nothing to do with the robberies. He's too busy taking care of everyone."

"Where does Andy's dad live?" he asked.

She shook her head.

"You don't know?"

"I didn't even know they had gotten divorced," she pointed out, and that guilt was in her voice again, as if she considered herself responsible, "so how would I know where either of them is living now?"

"One of them might have kept the house where they lived before Andy died," he said. "You know where that is."

He felt a flash of guilt that it might have been the house where Andy had grown up—a house where she and Andy had shared memories. It would be hard for her to go back to that.

"I know," she admitted and then confirmed his thoughts when she added, "but I don't want to go there."

He wished he didn't have to take her there. But he had to find Mark before his wife had a chance to warn him that a man, a friend of Maggie's, was looking for him. Because then the man would run for sure...

Blaine Campbell cared only about his job. He didn't care about her or he wouldn't have made her give him directions to Andy's childhood home in southwestern Michigan. He wouldn't have kept her in the car to go with him. He wouldn't have made her keep revisiting her past and her guilt.

Everything had fallen apart since Andy's death. And that was all her fault. If she had told him the truth earlier, he wouldn't have reenlisted. He wouldn't have needed the money for the damn ring she had never wanted.

Blaine Campbell had taken it as evidence against Susan Iverson. She hoped he never returned it.

Maggie stared out the windshield at the highway that wound around the Lake Michigan shoreline. She had always liked this drive—until she had traveled it up for Andy's funeral. Then she had vowed to never use it again.

She hadn't wanted to go back. It wasn't home without her best friend. She had to make a new home for herself and for her baby. But she was afraid that she hadn't found one yet—at least, not one where they would be safe.

"Andy's been gone awhile," Blaine remarked.

"Nearly six months," she said. But sometimes it hadn't sunk in yet. Sometimes she still looked for his letters in her mailbox or an email in her in-box or a call…

"Did you even know that you were pregnant when you learned that he'd died?"

She nodded. Since her cycle had always been so regular, she'd taken a test on her first missed day. She hadn't been happy with those test results because she'd known that Andy would insist on marrying her. He had always been so old-fashioned and so honorable. But now he was dead…

Blaine's gaze was on the road, so he must have missed her nod. She cleared her throat and replied, "Yes, I had just found out."

"You're strong," he said.

She nearly laughed. Had he already forgotten how she'd screamed her head off that first day they'd met? She wasn't nearly as strong as she'd like to be. If she was, she might have saved Sarge. "Why do you say that?"

"Some women might have lost the baby," he explained, "because of the stress."

"I was fine." She hadn't had any problems then; she hadn't even had morning sickness. She was more afraid of losing the child now.

As if he'd heard her unspoken thoughts, he reached across the console and squeezed her hand. "I'll keep you safe," he promised. "I'll keep you both safe."

Andy had made promises, too. He'd promised that he would return from his last deployment. So Maggie knew that some promises couldn't be kept. She suspected that the promise Blaine had just made was one of them.

He didn't believe that, though. He thought it was a promise he could keep and his green eyes were full of sincerity as he shared a glance with her. Then he turned his attention back to the road and to the rearview mirror. His hand tensed on hers before he released it and gripped the wheel.

"Hold on!" he warned her as he pressed harder on the accelerator.

Maggie instinctively reached out for the dashboard, bracing her hands against it, just as the SUV shot forward. "What's going on? Why are you driving so fast?"

She had felt safe with him earlier. But not now.

"Just hold on," Blaine said again, as he sped up some more.

Tires squealed as he careened around a curve.

"What are you doing?" she asked again—with alarm.

But then more tires squealed and metal crunched as another vehicle slammed hard into the rear bumper of the SUV. The SUV fishtailed, spinning out of control toward where the shoulder of the road dropped off to the rocky lakeshore below. Nobody had ever broken a promise to her as fast as Blaine just had.

Maggie screamed in fear as the SUV teetered on two tires, about to roll over and plummet to that rocky shore.

Chapter Eleven

Blaine cursed and jerked the wheel, steering the SUV away from the shoulder. Gravel spewed from the tires as the SUV fishtailed, the back end sliding toward that steep drop-off to the rocky shore below. He needed all four tires on the pavement before he could accelerate. But before he could regain complete control, the van struck again. Metal crunched on the rear door of the passenger's side.

Too close to Maggie and her baby.

He had just promised that he would protect them. It was a promise that he'd had no business making. As a marine, he knew that there were promises that couldn't be kept—the way all his fallen friends had promised their families they would come home again. It was a promise that Maggie's fiancé had probably made to her when he'd given her that ring.

Blaine was not about to break his promise. At least not yet.

He pressed on the accelerator, taking the curve at such a high speed that a couple of the tires might have left the asphalt again. The black cargo van skidded around the corner behind him, its tires slipping off the pavement onto the gravel shoulder. So close to that dangerous edge, the van slowed down, and Blaine increased the distance between them.

He had grown up driving on roads like this—roads that curved sharply around lakes. But there had been mountains to maneuver, too, in New Hampshire. So he wasn't fazed. But neither was the driver of the van as he regained control and closed the distance between them again.

Blaine wanted to reach for his gun; he wanted to shoot out the van's tires and windshield. He wanted to do anything he could to stop the van from slamming into them again. But he needed both hands on the wheel to keep the SUV from plummeting over the rocky shoulder, and he didn't want Maggie trying to use his weapon.

He didn't want Maggie doing anything but hanging on—especially as the van made contact with them again. But the SUV absorbed the impact better than the van did.

In the rearview mirror, Blaine caught sight of a dark cloud as smoke began to billow from beneath the hood of the vehicle behind them. The rear bumper of the SUV was probably mangled, but so were the front bumper and the grille of the van.

If the radiator was ruined, it wasn't going to get far. He could just wait for it to stop running and try to apprehend the driver and whoever else was riding with him. But Blaine had no idea how many people were inside the van or how much firepower they had.

Even if he hadn't just made that promise to protect them, he couldn't risk the safety of Maggie and the baby. So he accelerated again and took the curves at breakneck speed. Maggie's hands were still pressed against the dashboard as she braced herself and her baby for another hit.

But the van didn't catch up again.

Blaine slowed down and, using his cell, called in the attempt to run them off the road. He described the van and then he asked for the nearest hospital.

"Do you think one of them was hurt?" Maggie asked as she peered behind them. But the van was no longer in view.

It might be where Blaine had left it smoking. Or the driver might have turned it around and tried to get somewhere they could hide it—the way they had tried to hide the getaway van between those Dumpsters in the alley.

He doubted blood would be found inside this van. He hadn't been able to take any shots at them. So he explained, "I'm taking *you* to the hospital."

She shook her head. "I'm fine."

Her face was eerily pale, and he could see the frantic beat of her pulse pounding in her throat.

"No, you're not fine," he argued, as he followed the directions the local dispatcher had given him to the hospital.

If there was something wrong with her or the baby, it was his fault. He should not have brought her along with him. He hadn't been any better at protecting her than the young officer the night before. Even with the van chasing them, he should have driven more carefully.

He slowed down on his way to the hospital. But he wanted her checked out. He wanted to make sure that she and the baby were fine.

Before he left them...

BLAINE HAD INTENDED to leave as soon as a doctor had taken Maggie into the ER to be checked out. But before he could cross the waiting room to the exit doors, another FBI agent, badge dangling down the front of a black leather jacket, showed up at the hospital.

"Agent Dalton Reyes," the dark-haired man introduced himself, hand outstretched. He didn't look much like the proverbial men in black since he wore a jacket and jeans instead of a dark suit.

But Blaine wasn't wearing a suit, either—just black pants and shirt. Since interrupting the robbery in progress, he hadn't had an opportunity to even take his suits out of their dry-cleaning bags.

"Reyes?" Ash had mentioned the young agent before. The Bureau had recruited him from an undercover gang task force with the Chicago PD. "You work organized crime?"

The dark head bobbed in a quick nod. "Yeah. Right now I'm working on a car-theft ring. The black cargo van that just tried running you off the road was recovered. It's one these thieves grabbed yesterday. This ring is very organized and very professional. You put in a request, and they'll steal the vehicle you want."

Blaine had put out a request himself—for information on a ring just like this. "Thanks for getting back to me about this, but you could have just called…"

Reyes grinned. "I could've, but then I wouldn't have gotten a chance to meet the infamous Blaine Campbell."

"Infamous?" Blaine asked. He didn't think that adjective had ever been used for him before.

"You've got quite a reputation."

He groaned. "What has Ash told you?"

Dalton laughed. "Ash doesn't talk. But he's damn good at getting other people to talk."

He was new to the Chicago Bureau, so people were bound to talk about him. To wonder what his story was, to worry that he might move up ahead of agents who had been there longer. He didn't care to move into management; he just wanted to take criminals off the street. He had never wanted to put anyone away more than these suspects. They'd already killed Sarge and were determined to kill Maggie, too.

"How about you?" Blaine asked, turning the conversation back to what he really cared about: the case. "Can you get these car thieves to tell you who's been putting in the requests for these vans?"

"I've got an inside man," Dalton said. "So I've got confirmation that the bank robbers have been paying—and paying big—to get disposable vehicles for the bank heists."

"Who?" he asked. "Who the hell are these robbers?"

Dalton shrugged. "My guys aren't the kind who care about names. In fact, they would probably rather *not* know. The only thing they care about is cash."

Blaine cursed as frustration overwhelmed him. He needed a lead and some hard evidence. "Does your inside man at least have a description of the guy ordering the vans?"

"Good-looking guy with dark hair and light eyes," Dalton replied with a chuckle. "My inside man is actually a woman."

That description matched the man from the security footage—the man who'd lifted Maggie into his arms. "I'll send you a picture to see if she can confirm it's my guy."

Blaine would forward him a screen shot from the security cameras as well as Mark Doremire's DMV picture. If he was the man, Blaine could link him to the vans and therefore the robberies. Maggie would have to accept his involvement.

But then it would probably be like losing Andy again—to lose another piece of him when she realized his brother wasn't the man she'd thought he was.

He hadn't been checking up on her as his brother had requested. He'd been casing the banks where she worked.

Dalton nodded. "Send me the photo. I'll get it to my informant right away. Whatever you need to get these guys, let me know. I'm happy to help."

He obviously knew about Sarge. Blaine sighed. "Ash must've talked some."

Reyes nodded again. "Yeah. He said this one's personal for you both."

It was, but not just because of Sarge. It was personal because of Maggie, too.

"He thinks it might be extra personal for you, though," Reyes continued, "because of the witness."

He glanced toward the ER, where Blaine kept looking, wondering how Maggie and the baby were.

"Ash talks too damn much," he said.

Reyes chuckled. "He's worried about you. He thought I should tell you about another agent who works out of the Chicago Bureau, Special Agent Bell. He works serial killers."

"Maggie's not a serial killer," Blaine said. She was not a criminal at all. "She's a victim."

"Yeah, Bell got too *personally* involved with a victim's sister," Reyes said. "It's the case he never solved. The serial killer he never caught."

Would these suspects be the ones that Blaine never caught—because he cared too much?

"You can't go!" Maggie exclaimed as she clutched at Blaine's arm, panicking at the thought of being separated from him. Since the first moment she'd met him, she'd thought him a golden-haired superhero, and every time he saved her life he proved that he was her hero.

"There are local authorities here," he said, gesturing with his free arm to where two police officers stood near the nurses' station. "You'll be safe."

She shook her head in protest. He couldn't pass her off to someone else again. He couldn't leave her. She was afraid that she wouldn't be able to protect her baby without him. "I'm not safe anywhere. Except with you."

"Not even with me."

"You kept me safe," she said. "They were trying to run us off the road. We would have been killed if you hadn't driven the way you had."

His voice gruff, he brushed off her gratitude. "But I could have hurt you…"

"The doctor said that the baby and I are both fine," she reminded him. "I can leave now. They don't need to keep me for observation." Blaine was the only one who wanted her to stay in the hospital with the local deputies guarding her. "I can leave with you now."

He wouldn't meet her gaze, just shook his head. "I don't think that's a good idea."

"Why not?" she asked. "Where are you going? Have they found the van?" She'd seen the smoke from under the hood. It probably hadn't gotten very far.

"The van has already been recovered," he said. "Empty. And it had been stolen."

"So you're not going there," she said. "So where are you going?" That he didn't want her along. Had he found another lead he was pursuing? Was he going to put himself in danger?

The thought of that scared her as much as being without his protection. She didn't want anything happening to Blaine. Maybe it was just the danger and the fear that had her so attached to him, but she had never felt like this before. She had never been as drawn to another person.

"I'm going to Andy's dad's house," he said. "I confirmed that he is still living in the house where Andy grew up."

She hadn't wanted to go back there, now that Andy was gone. "I thought you wanted me to go along."

"I was wrong to even consider taking you there," he said. "It's too dangerous."

"It's Andy's dad—"

"And maybe his brother."

If they believed Tammy…

Maggie wasn't so sure that they should. While Mark had always been caring and friendly, sometimes too friendly, Tammy had always seemed cold to her—even at Andy's funeral. Maybe that was just because Mark had been too friendly.

But Tammy wasn't at the dad's house. "They're not going to hurt me," she said. "I've known his dad for years." But, truthfully, she hadn't known Andy's parents that well. They had usually hung out at her house or around town more than at Andy's.

"Maybe his dad wouldn't hurt you," Blaine said. "But you're wrong about his brother. The description of the guy who ordered the stolen vans matches Mark's description."

"Dark hair? Blue eyes?" She shrugged. "A lot of guys look like that." Except for Blaine. She had never seen a man as attractive as he was, but it wasn't just his looks. It was his protectiveness and his courage and his intelligence that she found even more compelling than his physical appearance.

"I sent someone a picture of Mark for a positive ID," he said.

"It won't be," Maggie said. She refused to accept that Andy's big brother could be robbing banks. "Mark wouldn't hurt me." He had promised Andy that he would take care of her. He would never break his promise to his brother.

Blaine sighed as if exasperated with her. Maybe that was why he wanted to leave her at the hospital. He was tired of her. "Don't you think it's strange that we were run off the road shortly after leaving his house?"

Her heart—that had finally slowed from a frantic beat—started pounding hard again. "No..." She really didn't want Mark involved. "That van could have followed us from the bank."

"I doubt it," Blaine replied. "I was too careful. I didn't see anyone following us. I think Mark was either in that house or his wife called him and told him where we were heading."

"But you didn't say where," she reminded him. "You said that we would come back to their house the next day. If they were involved, wouldn't they have just waited for us to come back?"

"Or they'll make damn sure they're gone before tomorrow." He pushed a hand through his disheveled blond hair. "Hell, they could be gone now. I have to go."

She didn't release his arm. "You can't go without me." She hadn't wanted to go back to Andy's house, hadn't wanted to relive the past. But now she was more afraid of the future. She didn't want to be separated from Blaine and she wasn't sure it was just because she was scared.

"I can't put you in danger again," he said.

"I won't be in any danger," she said. "This is Andy's family. I'm carrying Andy's baby. They're not going to hurt me." They wouldn't want to lose that last piece of Andy any more than she did.

His mouth curved into a slight grin. "What about me?"

"They're not bad people," she said. "They won't hurt you, either."

"That wasn't what I meant." He stared at her, his green

gaze tumultuous with regret. "I'm worried that I'm going to hurt you."

"You've saved my life again and again," she reminded him. She would never forget how he had protected her and her baby. Maybe gratefulness was the feeling overwhelming her and making her panic at the thought of him leaving her. But it didn't feel like just gratitude. "You're not going to hurt me."

Physically—he wouldn't. She knew that he would protect her from physical harm. He had proved that over and over again.

But he was only doing his job. And she had to remember that. She had to remember that, when he caught the robbers, Blaine would move on to his next assignment, and he would leave her.

For good.

So he probably would hurt her. Emotionally. If she let herself fall for him…

But she wouldn't do that. She wouldn't risk her heart on anyone right now. She was going to save all her love for her baby.

Chapter Twelve

Maggie was getting to him in a way that no one had ever gotten to Blaine before. He couldn't even draw a deep breath for the panic pressing on his chest.

What had he been thinking to bring her along? He shook his head in self-disgust.

"What?" she asked from the passenger seat of the battered SUV.

"I shouldn't have brought you…"

"I told you that I won't be in any danger."

Maybe she wouldn't be. But he was worried that *he* was in danger. He was in danger of falling for her. And that would be the biggest mistake he'd ever made.

It wasn't that he still believed she was involved in the robberies. But he would be a fool to totally rule out the possibility. Even though there were attempts being made on her life, it could be to silence her, so that she wouldn't reveal her coconspirators. But he doubted that. If she actually knew anything about the robbers, she would have told him by now; she was too scared to keep secrets any longer.

The reason it would be a mistake for him to fall for Maggie Jenkins was because she was in love with another man. He suspected she would forever love her dead fiancé.

That was why she had insisted on coming along with him. To protect Andy's family from him.

"I really don't believe they're involved," she insisted. And he wondered now if she was trying to convince herself or him.

"Andy could have told them what you had shared with him about the bank," he said. "What did you share with him?" And how did it tie in to the robberies?

"I rambled on," she said, "like I usually do since I talk so much. I complained about working harder than the manager. I told him what my duties were—how I handled the money deliveries and pickups—how I knew the security code for the back door and the vault."

That information had definitely been used in the robberies. Even at the other banks, the robbers had threatened the assistant managers and never questioned the managers.

"It sounds like Andy shared that information with his brother." And Mark had used it to rob all the banks.

She shook her head, tumbling her brown curls around her shoulders. "Andy wouldn't talk to anyone about my job."

"Why not?" he asked, and he wondered about her dismissive tone.

She shrugged. "It's not very interesting."

"It's not?"

"Most of the time it's very boring," she said.

Had Andy thought her job boring and uninteresting? "But you told him about it anyway?"

"I wrote about it," she said. "I guess my letters to him were kind of like writing in a journal. I complained about stupid policies and procedures."

"You wrote him letters?"

"Yes," she said. "Didn't I tell you that before?"

"Not about the letters—just that Andy was the only person you'd told about your job," he said. Because she told Andy everything. He'd thought that had been in person, though. "Where are the letters now? Did you get them back?"

She shook her head. "No. I don't know what would have happened to them after he...after he..." She trailed off, unable to talk of his death. Of her loss...

"His personal effects would have been returned to his family," Blaine said. He was definitely right about Andy's family; they had to be involved in the robberies.

Maggie sucked in a breath, as if she had just realized it, too. "But they wouldn't have read his personal letters..."

"If they miss him as much as you do," he pointed out, "they might have."

"But those are letters that *I* wrote to him," she said, her voice cracking with emotion. "They're not the letters he wrote to me. They're not about Andy and his life."

"I'm sorry," he said. She had every right to be angry. "Those letters should have been returned to you. They're your personal thoughts and feelings. Hell, you were his fiancée. You should have gotten everything."

She shook her head in denial. "We weren't married. So his personal effects should have gone to his family."

"You're family—you and his baby," Blaine said. "His parents and brother should have at least given you those letters."

"Maybe they just didn't have time..." She kept defending them.

Maybe she was naive. Maybe she just tried to see the best in everyone. But that was how she had wound up with Susan Iverson as a roommate. She didn't need protection just now; she needed it every day. She needed protection from her own sweetness and generosity.

"His brother's been checking on you," he said. The image from the security footage of him hugging her hadn't left his mind. "He could have brought the letters to you then. He's had six months to get them to you." Unless he had been using them for something else—to help him plan the bank robberies.

"We're here," she said with a sigh of relief as he pulled the battered SUV to the curb across the street from the brick Cape Cod.

He could have sworn earlier today that she hadn't wanted to come back here. Of course, she thought she was going to prove to him that Andy's family wasn't involved. But with every new thing he learned, his suspicions about them grew. He didn't even need confirmation from Dalton Reyes that Mark Doremire was the one ordering those stolen vans.

He was so convinced that Doremire was involved that he'd had a local officer watching the house before they arrived. The car was parked a little way down the street. Too far down the street if Doremire and his father were armed. The other men from the bank could be there, too.

Maggie reached for her door handle, but Blaine caught her arm and held her back from opening the door. With his other hand, he grabbed his cell and checked in with the officer.

"Nobody's come or gone, Agent Campbell," the officer assured him.

So what did that mean? That they had holed up in the house with weapons? At least the driver of the van, and whoever else might have been riding inside, couldn't have joined them. They wouldn't have had time to ditch the van for another vehicle and drive up without the officer seeing them.

Blaine clicked off the cell and turned back to Maggie. "I want you to stay here until I check out the inside of the house."

"Mr. Doremire may not let you in unless he sees me," she warned him. "Andy's parents kind of kept to themselves when we were growing up. They didn't socialize much. So he's not going to open his door to a stranger."

Blaine tugged his badge out of his shirt. He wasn't hiding it this time. "This will get him to open the door," he said. Or he would knock down the damn thing. "You need to stay here until I determine if it's safe or not."

He waited until she reluctantly nodded in agreement before he stepped out the driver's side. But moments later Mr. Doremire proved her right. When Blaine knocked on the door, a raspy voice angrily called out, "Go away!"

"I am Special Agent Campbell with the FBI," Blaine identified himself. "I need you to open up this door, sir. I need to talk to you about your son."

"It's too late for that!"

That was what Blaine was afraid of. That Mark was already gone—that he'd taken off to some country from which he couldn't be extradited. But then, who had tried running them off the road on the way here? Only Mark would have known they had stopped at his house looking for him. Only Mark would have known where they'd been heading.

"Go away!" the older man yelled again.

"Let me try," a soft voice suggested as Maggie joined him at the solid wood door to the Cape Cod. It was painted black—like the shingles on the roof. And there was no welcome mat.

"I told you to stay in the vehicle," he reminded her.

Even with the squad car not far away, she wasn't safe; someone could have taken a shot at her as she had crossed the street.

Ignoring him, she knocked on the door. "Mr. Doremire, it's me—it's Maggie. Please let us in…"

Inside the house, something crashed and then heavy footfalls approached the door. It was wrenched open, and a gray-haired man stared at them from bloodshot eyes.

Blaine could smell the alcohol even before the man spoke. "Have you heard from him?" he demanded to know.

"Mark has been by to see me," she said. "At the bank. Is he here?"

"Mark?" the older man repeated, as if he didn't even recognize the name of his eldest son. "I'm not talking about Mark."

Did the man have other boys? Maybe there were more Doremires involved than Blaine had realized. Maybe they made up the entire gang.

But Maggie's brow furrowed with confusion, and she asked, "Who are you talking about?"

"Andy," Mr. Doremire replied, as if she was stupid. "Have you heard from Andy yet?"

She reached out and clasped the older man's arm and led him back inside the house. "I'm sorry, Mr. Doremire," she said as she guided him back into his easy chair. A bottle of whiskey lay broken next to the chair. But no liquor had spilled onto the hardwood floor. He'd already emptied it.

She crouched down next to the old man's chair and very gently told him, "Andy's dead. He died in Afghanistan."

"No!" the gray-haired man shouted hotly in denial.

"He didn't die. That's just what he made it look like. He's alive."

She shook her head, and her brown eyes filled with sympathy and sadness. "No…"

"I've seen him," the man insisted. "He's alive!"

"No," she said again. "That's not possible. His whole convoy died that day. There's no way he survived." And her voice cracked with emotion and regret.

Mr. Doremire shook his head in denial and disgust. "That boy wasn't strong enough for the Marines," he said. "He had no business joining up. He got scared. He took off. He wasn't part of that convoy."

Why was Andy's father making up such a story? Just because he couldn't handle his son being dead?

"They wouldn't have reported that he was dead if they hadn't been certain," Maggie continued, patiently. "They wouldn't have put us through that and neither would Andy."

"None of the remains recovered have actually been identified, so there is no way of proving that he was part of the convoy," the older man insisted. "They never even recovered his dog tags."

"They are still working on DNA," Maggie said with a slight shudder. "But they know that Andy's gone…" And from the dismal sound of her voice, she knew it, too.

Blaine hated that she was reliving Andy's last moments. Or had those actually been his last moments? Was Andy's father right? Was Maggie's fiancé still alive? Mr. Doremire had claimed that he'd seen him.

If so, Blaine had another suspect for the robberies— one who had definitely read her letters and knew about the bank's policies and procedures, and the duties and responsibilities of the assistant manager.

"Will you be okay in here?" Blaine asked Maggie.

She nodded. "Of course."

But she stared up at him with a question in her eyes as if wondering where he was going…

"I have to make a call," he said.

From his years as a marine, he had connections, people he could call to verify if Andy Doremire had been identified among the convoy casualties. Maybe they hadn't identified the remains immediately after the explosion, but in the past six months they would have. And he couldn't trust that Mr. Doremire's drunken claims were valid. Or was Andy alive and robbing banks?

MAGGIE BIT HER bottom lip to stop herself from calling out for Blaine. She didn't want to be left alone with Andy's dad and his outrageous story. He was drunk, though. That had to be why he was talking such nonsense.

"He's calling someone in the military," Dustin Doremire said. "He's going to talk to some marines."

Blaine had been a marine. He would know whom to talk to.

"Probably," she agreed. "He's wasting his time, though." Andy was dead. Therefore, he was not robbing banks—as Blaine probably now suspected.

"They're not going to tell him anything," Mr. Doremire said with a derisive snort. "It's a cover-up."

So he was drunk and paranoid. "What are they covering up?" she asked. She wasn't even sure who "they" were supposed to be. First Andy had faked his death and now someone else was covering it up?

"You know what they're covering up," he accused her, suddenly turning angrily on her.

She edged back from his chair, not wanting to be so close to him. "I don't know what you're talking about." That was definitely the truth.

"Andy told you everything," he said. "You know…"

But now she wondered. Had Andy told her everything? He had never mentioned his father drinking so much. Maybe it had started only after his death. But now she wondered—because she hadn't come over to Andy's house very often. He had always come to hers. And if his car was broken down and she had to pick him up, he met her on the street.

Maybe she hadn't been the only reason Andy had joined the Marines. Maybe he hadn't done it just to support her, the way he had old-fashionedly claimed he'd wanted to do. Maybe he had also joined to escape his father.

"That boy loved you so much," Mr. Doremire continued. "He was crazy about you."

Andy had loved her. If only she could have loved him the same way…

The older man uttered a bitter laugh. "The boy was such a fool that he couldn't see you didn't feel the same way about him."

"I cared about Andy," she insisted. "He was my best friend." And she would forever miss him and she would regret that his son or daughter would never know him— would never know what a sweet guy he'd been.

"But you didn't love him," the older man accused her, as if she'd committed some crime. "It's your fault, girl. It's all your fault."

"What's my fault?" she asked.

"It's your fault he joined the Marines, trying to prove he was man enough for you." Mr. Doremire shook his head. "He wasted his time, too. You never looked at him like you're looking at that man…" He gestured toward where Blaine had gone out the open front door.

"That man is an FBI agent," she said. "He's investi-

gating the robberies at the banks where I've worked."
He had to have heard about the robberies; they'd made
the national news.

But the older man just stared bleary-eyed at her. Had
he even known she worked at a bank?

"I don't care who the hell he is," Mr. Doremire replied.
"He's not going to be raising *my* grandchild."

She hoped Blaine had stepped far enough away from
the open door that he hadn't overheard that. But her face
heated with embarrassment that he might have. She assured the older man, "Agent Campbell is not going to be
raising my child."

She knew that once the robbers were caught he would
move on to his next case. She was nothing more than a
witness and possible suspect to him.

"That's Andy's child!" Mr. Doremire lurched out of
the chair and reached for her as if he intended to rip the
baby from her belly.

She jerked back to protect her baby. She didn't even
want his hands on her belly, didn't want him hurting her
child—before he or she was born or after—the way he
must have hurt Andy had he ever spoken to him the way
he'd spoken of him.

"Mr. Doremire," she said, "please calm down." *And
sober up.*

"Andy won't be letting some other man raise his kid,"
he ominously warned her. "You'll see. He'll show himself to you, just like he's shown himself to me."

She wondered how many bottles of whiskey it had
taken for Andy to show himself. She suspected quite
a few.

"Andy is gone, Mr. Doremire," she said. "He's dead."
His hand swung quickly, striking her cheek before

she could duck. Tears stung her eyes as pain radiated from the slap.

"That's what you want," Mr. Doremire said. "You want him dead. But he's not! He's not dead!"

"Okay, okay," she said, trying to humor the drunk or deranged man. "He's alive, then. He's alive."

He had no idea how much she really wished that Andy was alive. Then she wouldn't have lost her best friend. She wouldn't feel so alone that she was clinging to an FBI agent who was only trying to do his job.

Maybe she was as crazy as Andy's dad to think that Blaine could have any interest in her beyond her connection to the bank robberies.

The older man started crying horrible wrenching sobs. "If he's dead, it's your fault," he said again. "It's all your fault!"

She nodded miserably in agreement. Maybe it was...

If he hadn't wanted to buy her that damn ring...

If he hadn't wanted to take care of her...

"You're the one who should be dead!" He swung his arm again.

And, realizing that the man wasn't just drunk but crazy, too, she cried out in fear that he might actually kill her.

Chapter Thirteen

Maggie's scream chilled Blaine's blood. He dropped his phone and ran back into the house—afraid of what he might find.

Why the hell had he left her alone? He hadn't even checked the house. Mark Doremire could have been hiding somewhere, waiting for his next chance to grab Maggie.

But when he burst into the living room, he found only the older Doremire and Maggie. She was backing up, though, and ducking the blows of the man's meaty fists.

Blaine jumped forward and caught the man's swinging arms. He jerked them behind his back. "Dustin Doremire, I am placing you under arrest for assault."

"No," Maggie said. "You don't need to arrest him." But her cheek bore a red imprint from the older man's hand.

Blaine jerked Doremire's arms higher behind his back, wanting to hurt him the way he had hurt Maggie. The old drunk only grunted. After all that whiskey, he was probably beyond the point of feeling any pain. Only inflicting it…

"He hurt you," he said. And Blaine blamed himself for leaving her alone with Andy's drunken father.

"He's hurting," she said, making excuses for the man's abuse. "He misses his son."

Blaine had placed a few calls. But nobody had really answered his questions about Andy Doremire. In fact, they'd thought he was crazy to even ask. Of course the man was dead. His family wouldn't have been notified if his death hadn't been confirmed.

Otherwise, he would have been listed as missing. Blaine knew that. But for some reason he had wanted to think the worst of Andy Doremire. He'd wanted proof that her dead fiancé wasn't the saint that Maggie thought he was—he wasn't a man worth loving for the rest of her life.

But he was a better man than Blaine was. Andy wouldn't have willingly left her alone and in danger.

"Are you all right?" he asked her. "How badly did he hurt you?"

She brushed her fingertips across her cheek and dismissed the injury. "It's nothing. I'm fine."

She wasn't fine. He could hear the pain in her voice. But he wasn't sure whether it was physical or emotional pain. He suspected more emotional. She hadn't wanted to come here—to Andy's childhood home. And now he understood why.

"He needs to be brought in," he said. "I need to arrest him." Actually he only intended to hand him over to the officer outside to make the arrest and process Mr. Doremire.

"Please don't," she beseeched him, her big brown eyes pleading with him, too.

"You never want me to arrest anyone," he said. "You make it hard for me to do my job." He had ignored her and arrested Susan Iverson anyway. He was tempted to do the same with Mr. Doremire. "I need to question him."

"Let *me* question him," she said.

He settled the older man back into his chair. The guy collapsed against the worn cushions. The chair was one of the only pieces of furniture left in the nearly empty house. In fact, the Cape Cod made Ash's little bungalow look almost homey.

Blaine had no intention of letting Maggie question him. But before he could ask, she already was. "When did you see Mark last?"

"Mark?" The older man blinked his bloodshot eyes, as if he had no idea whom she was talking about.

"Mark is your oldest son," she prodded him. "His wife, Tammy, said he was here—visiting you."

He shook his head in denial. "I haven't seen that boy for months. He's not like Andy. Andy keeps coming around to check on me."

Did he have his sons confused? Even Maggie thought they looked a lot alike. He shared a significant glance with her as they both came to the same realization.

"When was Andy here last?" she asked. "When did he come see you?"

Doremire's eyes momentarily cleared of the drunken bleariness, and he stared at her with pure hatred. "You have no right to say his name."

The old man would have reached out again; he would have swung his arm if Blaine hadn't squeezed his shoulder and held him down onto the chair.

"She has every right to say his name," Blaine insisted. "They were engaged."

The older man shook his head. "She never would've married him. She didn't care about him…"

"That's not true," Maggie said, but her voice was so soft she nearly whispered the words.

"She loved him," Blaine said. "You know that. You have the letters she wrote to your son. Where are they?"

The drunk blinked in confusion, the way he had when she'd asked about Mark. "Letters?"

"*My* letters," she said. "The ones I wrote to Andy when he was overseas. Do you have them?"

He shook his head. "His mother probably took them— like she took everything else when she left."

Blaine could see that she had taken most everything. And he could see why she had left, too, if the man had been like this with her. If he had been abusive...

"Where did Mrs. Doremire go?" Maggie asked.

"She took all Andy's life-insurance money and bought herself a condo."

That money should have gone to Andy's fiancée and his unborn child, but Andy must not have listed her as his beneficiary yet. Knowing she was carrying Andy's child, his family should have given her the money, though. It would have been the right thing to do.

But this family obviously didn't care about what was right. Or honorable. Or legal.

He had to find Mark Doremire—had to catch him before he got beyond Blaine's reach.

"Where is her condo?" Maggie asked.

Andy's father named some complex that had her nodding as if she knew where it was. "It's not that far from here," she said. "We can go there now."

Blaine had no intention of taking her anywhere but to a bed. To rest...

But the thought of a bed reminded him of that morning, of her flicking back the covers to reveal all her voluptuous curves. The woman was so damn sexy.

"Tell that witch that she didn't break me," Mr. Dore-mire said. "Tell her that I'm fine…"

He was anything but fine. The former Mrs. Doremire was probably well aware of that, though.

"I hope you will be," Maggie said. After how the man had treated her, how could she wish the best for him?

Blaine had met few women as sweet and genuine as Maggie Jenkins.

But the old man stared up at her again with stark hatred. "I hope you get what you deserve."

It wasn't so much what he said but the venomous tone with which he said it that had Blaine protesting, "Mr. Doremire—"

"And you, Mr. Agent, I hope the same for you. Maybe you two deserve each other…"

Blaine knew that wasn't true. Maggie deserved a better man. He should have protected her better than he had. So, finally, he guided her toward the door.

"But don't go thinking you're going to be raising that baby together," Mr. Doremire yelled after them. "Andy's going to take that baby. He's going to raise his son himself."

Maggie sighed. "Andy's gone…"

"He's not dead," the older man drunkenly insisted. "You're going to see when he comes for his baby boy. You're going to see that he's not dead."

Maybe he wasn't dead—in his father's alcohol-saturated mind or in Maggie's heart. Blaine wished he was man enough to deserve her love. But he suspected she had none left to give anyway.

ONCE BLAINE SAID it was too late to see Mrs. Doremire, Maggie feigned falling asleep in the SUV. She didn't want to talk. She didn't want to even look at Blaine. Her face was too hot, and not from Mr. Doremire's slap but with embarrassment over all the horrible things that old drunk had said in front of Blaine.

Maybe he hadn't heard everything; maybe he'd been outside during the worst of it. But he had come running back when she'd screamed. He had saved her—as he always did.

Mr. Doremire hadn't been wrong about how she looked at the FBI agent. Despite not wanting to fall for him, she was falling. She had more love to give than she'd realized. But Blaine wouldn't want her love—or anything else to do with her, for that matter—once the bank robbers were caught.

The SUV drew to a stop. Then the engine cut out. A door opened and then another. Hers.

Blaine slid one arm under her legs and another around her back, as if he intended to lift her up the way he would a sleeping child. She jerked back.

"Sorry," he said. "I didn't mean to scare you. I just didn't want to wake you up."

"I'm up," she said.

But he didn't step back; he didn't give her any room to step out of the SUV. He was too close, his green gaze too intense on her face.

Her skin heated and flushed. She wished he wouldn't look at her. She lifted her hand to her face.

But he beat her to it, bringing his hand up to cup her cheek. "I don't think it'll bruise," he said.

She shrugged. She couldn't have cared less about her face. The man's words had hurt far more than his slap. "It's fine."

"I'm sorry," he said.

"You're sorry?"

"I shouldn't have left you alone with him." Blaine pushed a hand through his disheveled hair. "I knew he was drunk. I never should have stepped outside."

"You called someone about Andy," she said. It wasn't a question because she knew that he'd done it. She had watched the new suspicions grow in his green gaze. "To make sure that he's really dead."

Finally he stepped back and helped her from the SUV. Then he escorted her from the street up to the little bungalow where they had spent the night before. He hadn't taken her back to the hospital or to a hotel.

Her chest eased a little with relief.

"Are you going to ask me what I found out?" he asked, opening the door.

She shook her head as she passed him and entered the living room. "No."

"So, you're sure he's dead?"

"I know it." Even before Mark had called her, she'd known. She'd seen the news of the explosion—of the casualties—and she had known Andy was among them.

"But they didn't even recover his dog tags," Blaine said.

She shrugged. "I don't know what was recovered or not. I don't know if my letters were even sent back. You should have let me talk to Mrs. Doremire."

"It's been a long day for you already," Blaine reminded her as he flipped on the light switch. "We went back to the bank and watched all that footage. Then we saw Mark's wife and nearly got run off the road."

She shuddered at the reminder of those harrowing moments when she had thought the SUV was going to flip over and crash onto the rocky shoreline.

"And if that wasn't already too much for you," he said, "then you were assaulted by a crazy drunk."

"He is crazy," she agreed. "Thinking that Andy's alive…"

"That makes sense, actually," Blaine said, "that he doesn't want to let his son go."

She sighed. "I guess that is his way of dealing with his grief—denial and alcohol."

"How about you?" he asked.

She stared up at him in confusion. She had dealt with her grief months ago and neither alcohol nor denial had been involved. "What do you mean?"

"Are you going to be able to let Andy go?"

"I don't think he's alive," she assured him. "I'm not seeing him anywhere." She didn't see ghosts. Regrettably, she did keep seeing zombies—in person and in her nightmares. She would probably rather see ghosts.

"That's not what I meant," he said.

"What did you mean?" she wondered.

Instead of explaining himself, he just shook his head. "It doesn't matter."

She thought that it might, though—to her. Did he want her to let Andy go? Or was he like her almost father-in-law and not entirely convinced that Andy was dead?

"What did the people that you called tell you?" she asked. She already knew, but she didn't want to leave him yet. As tired as she was, she didn't want to climb the stairs and go to bed. Alone.

"They said that Andy's dad's claims were crazy," he replied. "They're not covering up anything…"

"Mr. Doremire said a lot of crazy stuff," she said. Hoping to dispel her embarrassment, she continued, "Like that nonsense about us…"

"Nonsense?"

Her skin heated again and not just on her face; she was warm all over. "Of course. All his drunken comments about you and me. That was just craziness…"

"What was so crazy about it?" he asked.

She drew in a deep breath to brace herself for honesty. "It's crazy to think that you'd be attracted to me."

"It is?" That green gaze was intense on her face and then it slid down her body.

Now her warm skin tingled. "Of course it is," she said. "I'm so fat and unattractive…" And he was the most beautiful man she'd ever met.

"You're pregnant," he said. "And you're beautiful."

She laughed at his ridiculous claims; they were as outrageous as Mr. Doremire's. "I wasn't fishing for compliments. Really. I know exactly what I look like—a whale."

He laughed now as if she were trying to be funny. She had just been honest. He was not being the same as he replied, "I would not be attracted to a whale."

"You're not attracted to me." She wished he was. But it wasn't possible. Even if she wasn't pregnant, she knew he would never go for a woman like her—a woman who talked too much and didn't think before she let people get close to her.

He stepped closer to her, his gaze still hot on her face and body. "I'm not?"

She shook her head. But he caught her chin and stopped it. Then he tipped up her chin and lowered his head. And his lips covered hers.

Maybe he had intended the kiss as a compliment or maybe it was just out of pity. But it quickly became something more as passion ignited—at least in Maggie—and she kissed him back.

She locked her arms around his neck and held his head down for the kiss. Her lips moved over his before opening for his tongue. He plunged it into her mouth, deepening the kiss and stirring her passion even more.

Making her want more than just a kiss…

Chapter Fourteen

It had just been a kiss. But even though it had happened hours ago, Blaine still couldn't get it out of his mind. Probably because it hadn't been just a kiss. It had been an experience almost profound in its intensity.

And he hadn't wanted to stop at just a kiss. He had wanted to carry her upstairs to one of the bedrooms and make love to her all night long.

But he'd summoned all of his control and pulled back. His cell had also been ringing with a summons from the Bureau chief to come into the office for an update on the case.

"You've lost your objectivity," the chief was saying, drawing Blaine from his thoughts of Maggie.

"What? Why?"

"The witness," Chief Special Agent Lynch said.

Blaine glanced at the clock on the conference room wall. He had left her alone too long. Of course, he hadn't actually left her alone. He had left her with two agents guarding Ash's house—one patrolling the perimeter and one parked in a chair outside her bedroom door. They were good men, men for whom both Ash and Dalton Reyes had vouched. They weren't special agents yet; they were barely more than recruits. But Truman Jackson had been a navy SEAL and Octavio Hernandez had worked in the gang task force with Reyes.

She should be safe…

But he had thought that when he'd left the local authorities to protect her.

"The witness is in danger," he said. "That was proven today—" he glanced at the clock again and corrected himself "—*yesterday* when someone tried running us off the road."

"The van was processed."

"Any evidence?"

"Not like in the first one," the chief replied. "No blood."

"Have you gotten a DNA match yet?"

The chief shook his head. "We'll check some other databases—see if we can find at least a close match."

"Good—that's good."

"What leads have you come up with?" the chief asked. "Or have you been too busy protecting the *witness*?"

"She is the best lead," Blaine insisted.

"You checked to see if her fiancé is really dead," the chief said. "She's leading you to a dead man as a suspect?"

"She didn't think he was alive. It was the man's father who raised some questions…"

"You think her fiancé's family is involved in the robberies."

He sighed. "Her fiancé's brother is a viable suspect. Reyes even confirmed him as having bought the van recovered after the robbery. The one in which the blood was found." Someone else had ordered the black cargo van. Why? Was Mark already gone?

"Where is he?" the chief asked, as if he had read

Blaine's mind. "Why haven't you brought Mark Doremire in for questioning?"

"We haven't found him yet."

"We?" the chief asked. "You're having the witness help you do your job?"

"I have an APB out on him," he said. "The witness is helping me figure out places where the man could be hiding. We checked out his dad's house."

The chief studied him through narrowed, dark eyes. "So you're only using her to lead you to a suspect?"

Blaine tensed as anger surged through him. "I'm not using her. I'm trying to keep her and her baby from getting killed."

"Is it the pregnant thing that's getting to you?" the chief asked.

If this was the way this chief ran this Bureau, Blaine wasn't sure he would want to stay in Chicago after all. And he'd considered staying here, putting down roots. Chicago wasn't that many miles from his sister Buster, who had settled in west Michigan.

"What?" he asked, offended that his professionalism was being questioned.

"I've read your history. I know you have a few sisters. Is that it?" the chief persisted.

He didn't feel at all brotherly toward Maggie Jenkins. And he suspected that neither did Mark Doremire. "The robbers keep trying to grab her. One of these times that they're trying, we'll be able to catch them."

"So you're using her as bait."

He tensed again. Furious and offended. "You may have read my file, but you don't know me."

"Ash Stryker does," the chief said. "He vouched for you. Says you're the best."

Although Blaine appreciated his friend's endorsement, he added, "My record says that."

"I'm still worried about the witness."

So was Blaine.

"You no longer think she's personally involved in the robberies?" the chief asked, as if he wasn't as convinced.

"She didn't plan the robberies." Blaine was certain of it. "She didn't recruit the other robbers."

"What evidence do you have of that?" Chief Lynch asked. "Her word?"

"The attempts on her life," he replied.

"Coconspirators have never tried killing each other?" The chief snorted. "You've been doing this job long enough to know better than that."

"No honor among thieves," Blaine murmured.

"Or loyalty."

"If that were true, she would have given them up," Blaine pointed out. "If she knew who they were, the fastest way to stop them would be to tell me who they are."

"You really believe that she doesn't know?"

He nodded. "But the robbers don't realize she doesn't. They must think that she can identify them somehow. That's why she's our best lead to them. It's also why she's in so much danger."

"But guarding her isn't the best use of *your* time or talents," the chief said. "We'll put other agents on her protection duty. We can keep Jackson and Hernandez on her."

Blaine was used to butting heads with local authorities trying to run his investigation. Usually the Bureau respected his handling of a case. But maybe the chief was right. Maybe he had lost all perspective where Maggie Jenkins was involved.

Maybe it would be better for him to trust her protection to someone else…because he couldn't trust himself where Maggie Jenkins was concerned.

BLAINE HAD BEEN gone so long—all night and all morning—that Maggie doubted he was ever coming back. And she felt sick to her stomach because of it. Maybe that was why the baby was restless; maybe it was because he missed him, too.

Him? Andy's dad had called him a boy. Sometimes she thought her baby was, too. But she didn't care if she had a boy or girl; she just wanted a healthy baby. That was all she wanted.

She didn't want Blaine Campbell. *Liar,* she chastised herself. She had wanted him, the night before, when he'd kissed her senseless. But when he'd pulled back, and her senses had returned, she'd recognized his kiss for what it was. A balm for her battered ego. Pity…

So she didn't want Blaine Campbell anymore. All she wanted was a healthy baby. And she couldn't have that with someone trying to kill her. So she gathered her courage and picked up the phone one of the agents had let her borrow. She dialed a number she had looked up online. Andy's mom was listed.

"Hello?" a friendly female voice answered on the first ring.

"Mrs. Doremire?"

"Maggie? Is that you?" the older woman asked. "Is everything all right? Is the baby all right?"

"Yes." For now…

"Oh, thank God." The woman released a sigh of relief that rattled the phone. "What can I help you with, honey?"

Honey. She didn't hate her like Andy's dad did? "I stopped by your old home yesterday…"

The woman drew in a sharp breath. "I'm sorry that you did that. Was it...unpleasant?"

Maggie's cheek hadn't bruised, but it was still sensitive to the touch. "I understand that he's very upset about Andy's death."

"What death?" she asked.

And that sick feeling churned harder in Maggie's stomach. Was Andy's entire family crazy?

"My ex-husband refuses to accept that Andy's dead," Janet Doremire continued.

"Is that why he's drinking so much?"

"It's his new excuse to drink," Janet replied. "But he always had one."

Why had Andy never told her what he'd gone through at home? They had been best friends. But apparently neither of them had really told each other everything.

"I'm sorry..."

"He refuses to accept Andy's death because then he'll have to admit his blame for it."

"Blame?" Someone besides her blamed himself for Andy's death?

"He's the reason Andy joined the Marines," Janet explained. "Dustin told him that it would make a man of him."

But Maggie and Sarge had been right. Andy hadn't had the temperament for it. He wasn't like Blaine Campbell, who hadn't hesitated over firing his weapon or risking his life.

Mrs. Doremire sighed again. "Instead it killed him."

Was that why Andy's mom had left his dad? Because she blamed him, too? Or was it over the drinking? Maggie didn't want to pry.

But Mrs. Doremire willingly divulged, "Andy's death showed me that life's too short to waste. I wasted too many years with my ex. I didn't want to spend another minute in that unhappy marriage. Andy would have wanted me to be happy."

"Yes, he would have," Maggie agreed. He had loved his mother very much. But now she realized he had never said that much about his father.

"Andy would have wanted you to be happy, too," Janet Doremire continued.

Tears stung Maggie's eyes, but she blinked hard, fighting them back. He would have wanted her to be happy because that was the kind of man he'd been.

"I know you're carrying his baby, but you need to move on, Maggie," Janet Doremire continued. "You and Andy only ever dated each other. You got too serious way too young—like me and Andy's father had. You should get out there." The woman chuckled. "Well, once the baby's born."

"Mrs. Doremire, I can't—" Maggie couldn't have this discussion with Andy's mother. She couldn't talk about dating someone else. "That's not why I called you…"

"I'm sorry, honey," Mrs. Doremire said. "Why did you call me?"

"I was wondering if you had the letters I wrote to Andy—if they'd been returned in his personal effects…?"

"I don't know," Mrs. Doremire said. "I never looked through his stuff."

"Do you have it?"

"No. I left it and the rest of my past at the old house. I don't want to wallow in it. You shouldn't, either," Mrs. Doremire said. "You don't need those letters, honey. Let them and Andy go."

The baby shifted inside Maggie, kicking, as if in protest. Would Mrs. Doremire even want anything to do with her grandchild once he or she was born? Or was she determined to forget everything about Andy?

That was obviously her way of dealing with her grief. And Andy's dad chose to wallow in alcohol. Since his ex hadn't taken everything, as he'd claimed, he must have either broken it or sold it. What had he done with her letters?

"Thank you, Mrs. Doremire…" But she spoke only to a dial tone. The older woman had already hung up. "But I really do need those letters…"

"We just need to know who has them," a deep voice remarked.

She turned to find Blaine standing in her bedroom doorway. She hadn't even heard him open the door. How long had he been there?

"She says her ex-husband," Maggie replied with a sigh. "I don't want to go back there, but I really want those letters."

"I'll send an agent with a warrant for Andy's personal effects," he said. "We'll get them."

Her face heated with embarrassment. "I wish nobody had to see those letters."

"Nobody cares about the personal parts," Blaine said. "Just the parts that relate to the bank procedures."

"That's what I worry about someone reading," she admitted. "I was such a fool to share those details with anyone. I'll probably get fired when it gets out that it's all my fault."

"We don't know that it is," Blaine said. "Maybe nobody read those letters. And as you've pointed out, other banks were robbed."

"Other banks that probably follow the same procedures we do," she said with a sigh. "I'll get fired and be unable to get a job anywhere else." And then how would she support herself and her baby?

"Don't panic," Blaine said. "We'll figure this out."

No, he would. And once he figured it out, he would be gone.

"Where have you been?" she asked. Then her face grew hotter as she realized she sounded like his wife or girlfriend, like someone who actually had a right to ask him where he'd been.

"Bureau chief wanted an update on my progress," he replied easily, as if he felt she had a right to ask.

"You were gone a long time," she said. "You must've had a lot to tell him." He had probably told the chief about her letters and Andy's brother and dad.

"He had a lot to say, too," Blaine said with a sigh. "He thinks that I'm losing my objectivity where you're concerned."

"Because he thinks you should still consider me a suspect?" Maybe Blaine did; he had never really said that he no longer had any suspicions about her.

"Chief Lynch thinks that I shouldn't be the one protecting you," he said.

That explained the other agents who'd guarded her last night and today. But the thought of losing Blaine's protection panicked her. She wasn't just frightened for the baby's safety or hers; she was panicked at the thought of no longer seeing Blaine. "I don't understand. You've saved me. You've kept me safe."

"He's right," Blaine said. "I should not be protecting you. I have lost my focus."

"So you're going to send me away—to one of those *safe* houses again?" She was losing him already. She had been right to not fall for him. But despite her best intentions, she was afraid that it was already too late.

"Not yet," he said. And he stepped inside the room and closed the door behind himself. "Not tonight…"

"Blaine…?"

"This is why I shouldn't be the man protecting you," he said, "because I want you. Because I'm attracted to you, and when I'm around you, I can barely think, let alone keep you safe."

She must have fallen asleep; she must have been dreaming—because he couldn't be saying what she was hearing. Testing her reality, she reached out and touched his face. His skin was stubbly and sexy beneath her palm, making her fingers tingle.

"You're attracted to me?"

"I showed you last night," he reminded her, "with that kiss."

"I thought that was pity."

He laughed. "That wasn't pity."

"Then why did you stop?" She'd lain awake all night— wanting him. Needing him…

"I thought I was taking advantage of you," he said, "of your vulnerability."

She shook her head. "You weren't…"

"I want to," he said. "I want you…"

She wanted him, too, so she tugged him down onto the bed with her. And she kissed him with all the desire he had awakened in her the night before—all the desire she had never felt before. It coursed through her again as their lips met.

He kissed her back. And it was definitely not with pity but with desire. He touched her, too, his hands moving gently over her body.

Her pulse pounded madly. She wanted him to rip off her clothes, but he removed them carefully, slowly, as if giving her time to change her mind.

She had never wanted anything—anyone—more. She didn't take off his clothes slowly; she nearly tore buttons and snaps in her haste to get him naked. When all his golden skin was bare, she gasped in wonder at his masculine beauty. His body was so sleek but yet so muscular, too.

He made love to her reverently, moving his lips all over her body. He kissed her mouth, her cheek, her neck before moving lower. He nibbled on her breasts, tugging gently on her nipples.

She moaned in ecstasy, her body already pulsing with passion. She pushed him back on the bed and he pulled her on top of him, gently guiding his erection inside her.

"This is all right?" he asked, his hands holding her hips—holding her up before she took him all the way inside her. "For the baby?"

She bit her lip and nodded. Even though she had told her doctor it wouldn't be an issue, the female obstetrician had assured Maggie that sex wouldn't jeopardize her pregnancy at all. "It's fine."

He pulled her down until he filled her. And she moaned again.

"Are you okay?" he asked.

"Not yet," she said, as she began to move again—rocking back and forth—trying to relieve the inexplicable pressure building inside her. "But I will be…"

He helped, guiding her up and down—teasing her breasts with his lips and gently with his teeth—until ecstasy shattered her and she screamed his name. Then he thrust and called out as he joined her in ecstasy.

She collapsed on top of him, their bodies still joined. He clasped her to him, holding her tightly in his arms. His heart beat heavily beneath her head, and his lungs panted for breath. Finally his heart slowed and his breathing evened out, and she realized he'd fallen asleep beneath her.

She would have been offended if she wasn't aware that he'd had no sleep the past two nights. And maybe even more nights before that. She hadn't had much more sleep, so she began to drift off, too.

Until her eyes began to burn and her lungs…

At first she blamed guilt. But Mrs. Doremire was right. Andy would have wanted her to be happy, so she couldn't use him as an excuse. But as it became harder for her to breathe, she realized what the real problem was.

Smoke. Someone had set the house on fire.

Chapter Fifteen

"Blaine!"

The sound of his name—uttered with such fear and urgency—jerked him awake as effectively as if she'd screamed. He coughed and sputtered as smoke burned his throat and lungs.

Soft hands gripped his shoulders, shaking him. "The house is on fire! We have to get out!"

They pulled on clothes in the dark and Blaine grabbed up his holster and his gun. He couldn't believe that he hadn't awakened earlier. The fire must have been burning for a while because there was a lot of smoke—so much that it was hard to breathe. Hard to see. But there wasn't much heat.

Maybe the smoke was just a ruse to get them out of the house—where Maggie could be grabbed. Or shot. But the smoke, growing denser and denser, could kill her, too.

She coughed and sputtered. But she didn't speak. She must have been too scared.

So was Blaine. He was scared that he had failed her and the baby—that he had broken his promise to her that he would keep them safe. He shouldn't have let his desire for her distract him. He shouldn't have crossed the line with a material witness.

"We have to stay low," he said as he helped her down

to the floor. He reached forward and touched the door, his palm against the wood. It wasn't warm—at least, not as warm as the floor beneath his knees.

Maggie must have felt it, too, because she gasped and started to rise. But Blaine caught her arm and pulled her back down as she began to cough.

Getting out wouldn't be easy, especially if the whole first floor was engulfed as he suspected. But he didn't have time to devise a plan. He had to act now—before the floor gave way beneath them.

So he opened the door to the hall. The smoke was even thicker than in the bedroom. He crossed it quickly to the bathroom, grabbed towels from a shelf and soaked them under the tub faucet. Maggie was still in the hall as if she hadn't been able to see where to go. He wrapped Maggie's face and body in the wet towels, and then he picked her up in his arms.

"Blaine..."

He coughed, and his eyes teared up from the smoke. But there was no time. And maybe there was no escape. He couldn't jump out a second-story window—not without hurting Maggie and her baby. So he ran toward the stairs. The bottom floor was aglow from the flames, but none licked up the steps. So he ran down them—wood weakening and splintering beneath them from the heat and the fire.

The house creaked and groaned as the flames consumed it. And the smoke overwhelmed him, blinding him to any exits. But he remembered where the front door was.

But had it been barricaded? Or were those gunmen waiting outside it to make sure they didn't escape?

As he headed toward it, the door burst open, and men in masks hurried into the house. These weren't those horrible zombie masks. These masks had oxygen pumping into them and were attached to hats. Firemen had arrived. Of course one of Ash's neighbors would have called the police. They would have noticed the flames—unlike Blaine.

He shouldn't have sent the other agents away. But he had wanted one last night alone with Maggie. That night might have cost her life or her baby's life. Her body was going limp in his arms.

One of the firemen took Maggie from him and carried her out. Blaine should have fought the man. He should have made certain that he really was a fireman. What if it was one of the robbers in another disguise?

Blaine hurried after him, but the smoke was so thick in his lungs now that he couldn't draw a breath deep enough. He couldn't breathe. And before he could hurry after Maggie, the house shuddered as the second story began to fall into the first...

MAGGIE'S THROAT BURNED. From the smoke and from screaming. Over the fireman's shoulder, she had seen the roof collapse and the house fold in on itself...and on Blaine. She'd pounded on the fireman's shoulders, but he hadn't released her.

And for a moment, she had stared up in fear that the mask wasn't any more real than the zombie masks had been. She'd worried that it had just been a disguise.

And she'd reached for it. But she'd been too weak to pull it off. Too weak to fight off the man as he carried her away. He put her into the back of a vehicle, and it sped away with her locked inside. Sirens wailed and lights flashed, but she still did not trust where it would take her. She didn't trust the oxygen either that a young woman gave her in the back of that van.

What if it was a drug or a gas? What if it knocked her out? She tried to fight it, but she didn't have the strength to pull off the mask. And then it began to make her feel better, stronger.

So when the doors opened again, she was strong enough to fight. To run. But the doors opened to a hospital Emergency entrance. She pulled off the oxygen mask and asked, "Where's Blaine?"

The paramedic stared down at her as she pushed the stretcher through the sliding doors of the ER entrance. "Who?"

"Agent Campbell," she said. "He was in the house…" She coughed and sputtered, but she wasn't choking on the smoke. She was choking on emotion. "He was in the house…when the roof caved in…"

The paramedic shrugged. "I don't know…"

"Do you know if anybody else got out?"

Blaine hadn't been the only one inside; there had been other firemen, too. Real firemen, she realized they were. They would have saved him. Right? They would have made certain Blaine got out alive.

"I don't know, miss," the female paramedic replied. "We were told to get you to the hospital right away because of the baby."

Maggie had one hand splayed across her belly, feeling for movement. Was he okay? She hoped the smoke hadn't hurt him. She was scared to think of what it might have done to his heart. His brain…

"That's good," she agreed. "We need to check out the baby."

"And you, too," the paramedic said. She leaned back as doctors ran up.

But Maggie grabbed the young woman's arm. "Was

there another ambulance there?" Was there someone who could help Blaine?

Because after seeing the roof collapse, she had no doubt that all of the people still inside would need medical help. Maggie was glad that she and her baby had been brought to the hospital so quickly. But she also wished they would have waited for Blaine—to bring him in with her.

Then she would know how badly he'd been hurt. Or if he had survived at all…

The young paramedic didn't have a chance to answer her question before doctors and nurses whisked Maggie's stretcher into a treatment area. They hooked her to another oxygen machine and an IV. There was also a heart monitor for the baby and an ultrasound.

She breathed a sigh of relief when she heard the fast but steady beat. "He's alive…"

"His heart sounds good," a doctor agreed.

"And his lungs?"

"Did you ever lose consciousness?" someone asked. "Did you pass out from the smoke?"

Maggie shook her head.

"We'll administer some prenatal steroids to help the development of his lungs," the doctor said, "to make sure everything's fine…"

But everything wouldn't be fine until she learned if Blaine had made it out of the burning house.

"He's active," the doctor said as he watched the ultrasound screen.

He. The picture on the ultrasound confirmed what Maggie had previously only suspected. She was carrying a baby boy. She wanted to share that news with her best friend. But he was gone. She wanted to share that news with the man she loved. But Blaine was gone, too.

Maybe the IV contained a sedative because she must have drifted off despite her worry. She didn't know how much time had passed, but when she awoke, she was no longer in the emergency department. She was alone in a room but for the man—tall and broad-shouldered—who stood in the doorway.

Hope burgeoned in her heart. "Blaine?"

The man stepped forward…into the light that glowed dimly from another doorway, perhaps to the bathroom. The man's hair was dark and his eyes were light, not gold and green like Blaine's. Disappointment made her heart feel heavy in her chest. "You're not Blaine."

But the man who had purchased those stolen vans had been described as dark haired with light eyes. This man matched that description as much as Mark Doremire had.

Could he be one of the robbers? And if he'd forgone the zombie mask, then he had no intention of letting her live.

"Who are you?" she asked. She didn't recognize him. She would have had no way of identifying him as one of the suspects in the robbery.

"I'm not Blaine Campbell," he agreed with a short chuckle. "My name is Ash Stryker. I'm also an FBI agent and a friend of Blaine's."

"Is he okay?" she asked. "Is he here?" She struggled to sit up, ready to jump out of bed and go to him.

Ash shook his head. "No. He's not here. That's why he asked me to stay with you."

"But is he okay?" she asked, and her panic grew. Had Blaine asking Ash to stay with her been his deathbed request? Was that why he wasn't there?

Because he was gone? Dead and gone?

Ash nodded, but he had that same telltale signal of stress that Blaine did. A muscle twitched in his cheek.

Maybe that twitch wasn't just betraying his stress but his lie—like a gambler's tell in a poker game.

"No," she said, her voice cracking as hysteria threatened. "I don't believe you. I saw the roof collapse. He couldn't have gotten out of there without some injuries."

Serious injuries.

Fatal injuries.

The man flinched as if he'd felt Blaine's pain. "He has some bumps and scratches," he admitted. "And a couple of small burns. But he's fine. Or I wouldn't be here."

Even though Blaine had asked him? But then, he would have been too distraught over the loss of his friend to worry about her.

Maybe Blaine wasn't gone.

The dark-haired man sighed. "Of course, I have no place to go right now…"

"It was your house he was staying at," she realized. And that Blaine had let her stay at, as well. He should have taken her to a motel. It might not have protected her, but it would have protected Ash Stryker's house. "I'm sorry…"

"It wasn't your fault," he assured her.

"But whoever set the fire is after *me*," she said. "So I feel responsible." She felt responsible for the house and for those injuries Blaine had suffered. How badly had he really been hurt?

Agent Stryker moved closer to the bed and assured her, "You're not responsible for any of this."

"I wish that was true," she said. "I shouldn't have stayed at your house. I shouldn't have stayed with Blaine." Or made love and fallen in love with Blaine.

He chuckled. "Blaine was right…"

"What was he right about?"

"He said that you couldn't possibly have anything to

do with the robberies," Ash said. "He said that you're too good a person to be consciously involved."

He thought she was a good person?

"I figured Blaine was only thinking that because he grew up with sisters and has this whole chivalry thing going on," Ash said.

She nodded. "He is very chivalrous and protective." The man was a hero like she had never known.

"I also guessed that you're pretty," he said.

She didn't feel pretty now. She felt bedraggled from the smoke. Maybe it was good that Blaine wasn't there. He would have regretted sleeping with her.

Maybe he did regret it. Maybe that was why he wasn't here—with her. Had he even checked on her?

"Where is Blaine?" she asked.

Ash sighed. "He's determined to end this," he said. "He wants these guys caught."

"He wants to avenge Sarge's death," she said. "Sarge is—"

"I knew Sarge, too," Ash said with a grimace of regret and loss. "He was also my drill instructor."

"I'm sorry."

"Stop apologizing," he said. "None of this is your fault. Blaine is going to prove that. He's going to find out who the hell is responsible and bring them to justice."

She breathed a small sigh of relief. He had to be okay, then. He had to be strong enough to want revenge. But her breath caught again as she realized that he was putting himself in more danger.

"You should be with him," she said. "You should make sure he's really all right. The doctors wanted to keep me here because they're worried about my lungs having a delayed reaction to all that smoke. I think it's called hypoxia." That was why they were keeping her on oxygen.

Blaine wouldn't have oxygen with him. He wouldn't have anyone to help him if hypoxia kicked in, depriving his body of oxygen. He could die.

He wasn't just in danger from whoever was trying to kill them. He was in danger from his own body shutting down on him.

That muscle twitched in Ash's cheek again. He was worried, too. Blaine must have checked himself out against doctor's orders.

"Have you heard from him?" she asked.

He shook his head.

Maybe it was already too late to help Blaine.

Chapter Sixteen

Maggie was okay. So was her baby. Blaine hadn't left the hospital until he'd learned that. He hadn't left the hospital until Ash had shown up. He wouldn't have trusted anyone else to protect her. He probably shouldn't have trusted Hernandez and Jackson since he wasn't sure how the robbers had discovered where Maggie was staying.

He'd been so careful to avoid being followed—to avoid anyone discovering where he had hidden her. But he hadn't kept her safe. Ash would. Or at least he would try…the way Sarge had tried.

Maggie was in too much danger. She and her baby had survived this time. But eventually their luck would run out.

Blaine had to focus on finding the robbers. He couldn't think about her—or what they'd done right before the fire started. He couldn't think about anything but suspects.

He was determined to find the one who had so far eluded him. So he went back to Mark Doremire's house.

His wife opened the door and stared at him through eyes wide with surprise. At first he thought it might have been because of the hour; it was barely dawn. But she was looking at him instead of the sky.

"Are you all right?" she asked.

He felt as if a roof had fallen on him. But then, it had.

He'd been fortunate to come out with only a few scrapes and light burns. The firemen had used their own bodies to protect him. His lungs burned, though, from all the smoke he'd inhaled. The doctor hadn't authorized him to leave the hospital. He'd wanted to keep Blaine for observation—something about a delayed reaction to smoke inhalation.

But Blaine felt time running out since each attack on Maggie had been harder for her and for him to survive. So he had refused to stay and checked himself out against the doctor's orders.

"No, I'm not fine," he admitted. "I'm about to arrest you for obstruction of justice if you don't tell me where your husband is hiding."

She shrugged but continued to block the doorway to the kitchen the best she could with her thin frame. "I can't tell you what I don't know."

He could have pushed her aside and searched her house. But he'd had someone watching it—someone with thermal imaging who'd detected only one person inside the house. Mark really wasn't there. "You don't know where your husband is?"

She shook her head. "I figured he was following Maggie around like his brother used to. But it seems as though you're doing that now."

"I'm just doing my job," he said. But it was a lie. Protecting Maggie had less to do with his job than with his heart. He had fallen for her.

And just as Dalton Reyes and his boss had warned him, he'd gotten distracted. Because of that, he had nearly lost his life and hers, as well. He had to put aside his feelings for her and focus only on the case. He wasn't going to be like Special Agent Bell and leave this case unsolved.

The younger Mrs. Doremire snorted derisively as she recognized his lie. "So you've let sweet Maggie get to you, too," she said. "Something about her makes a man feel more important, more manly. That's what killed Andy. That dumb kid actually thought he could be a soldier—for her."

"That was Andy," Blaine said. "What about his brother? He's *your* husband." He wanted to goad her—to piss her off at Mark—so that she would give up his whereabouts.

"But I don't need him like dear sweet Maggie does," Tammy replied. "It doesn't help that before Andy left for his last deployment he asked Mark to watch out for her. Why do you think we moved here?"

Blaine shrugged even though he could have guessed. The robberies…

"Because she moved here," Tammy said. "I left behind my friends and family for Maggie."

"You hate her."

She laughed. "That's the thing about Maggie. You can't hate her. She's too sweet. But she's also manipulative as hell. She'll suck you in and ruin your life."

"Has she ruined yours?" he asked, wondering why the woman resented her so much.

"She ruined my marriage. I haven't seen Mark in days," she said. So she blamed Maggie for all the problems in her marriage instead of blaming her husband. "I have no idea where he is. So if you want—arrest me. Take me in for questioning. Drug me with truth serum. I'm not going to be able to tell you what I don't know."

"Who would know where he is?" Blaine wondered.

Tammy sighed and leaned wearily against the doorjamb. Her red hair was tousled, and she wore a robe. But somehow he doubted she'd had any more sleep than he had. "Like me," she said, "Mark left his friends behind in Michigan. Maybe his mom or dad would know where he's gone."

"His dad only talks about Andy," Blaine admitted.

"Everybody loved Andy. He was sweet—like Maggie," she said. "But genuinely sweet. He was a good man who died too soon."

"What about Mark?" he asked. "Is he a good man?"

She shrugged again.

"Could he be involved in the bank robberies?"

She gasped in surprise.

He narrowed his eyes skeptically at her surprise. "You didn't figure out that's why I'm looking for him?"

"I had no idea why you're looking for him," she said. "I thought you were just a friend of Maggie's."

He was so much more than just friends with her.

"I'm a special agent with the FBI," he said. "And I'm working the bank robberies—the one where the suspects wear zombie disguises."

She sighed. "Mark wouldn't have gotten involved in the robberies on his own." She laughed now. "God knows he's no criminal mastermind. He would have only gotten involved because someone asked him—or manipulated him—into getting involved."

He suspected what she would say next, on whom she would place the blame, but still he had to ask, "Who?"

"Maggie, of course."

"You think she's a criminal mastermind?" He could have laughed, too, at that thought. Not that Maggie wasn't smart. She was. She was also too honest and open to take anything from anyone.

She hadn't even been willing to take a compliment from him. But then she'd taken his desire—his passion. She'd made love with him, too.

"I think she's a desperate single woman who's about

to be raising a baby alone," Tammy Doremire said. "She just might be desperate enough to start stealing."

He doubted Maggie Jenkins was a bank robber.

And Mrs. Doremire must have seen that doubt because she added, "She's not above stealing, Agent. Even you think she probably stole my husband."

He doubted that, too. She thought of Mark as an older brother. But maybe Mark didn't think of her as a little sister. Maybe he saw her for the sweet, desirable woman that Blaine did.

He pressed his business card into the woman's hand. "If you see your husband, give me a call. I need to talk to him."

"If anyone knows where he is," she said, "it'll be Maggie. You should ask her where he is."

"If Maggie knew where he was, I wouldn't be here," he said with certainty. He had wasted his time talking to her.

Tammy Doremire glanced down at the card he'd handed her, then called after him when he started walking toward his SUV, "Be careful, Agent Campbell. The most danger you're in is from Maggie Jenkins."

He couldn't argue with her because he suspected she was right. Maggie was dangerous to him—to his heart. But somebody else was a danger to her, and Blaine wouldn't be able to leave her until he found out who and stopped that person.

"If you don't find him, I will," Maggie threatened as she struggled to escape her bed. But the oxygen line tugged at her nose and face. And the IV held her like a manacle.

Ash stretched out his hands, as if trying to hold her back. "Maggie, you have to stay here for observation."

"*You* don't," she said. "Go find him."

"I'm here for observation, too," Ash said. "I'm here to observe you."

"I don't need observation," she said. "I need to know that Blaine is really all right. And if you won't find out for me, I will find out myself." She struggled to sit up again.

"Blaine will kill me if I leave you," Ash said. "I promised him I'd watch out for you."

"Have someone else stand outside the door," she suggested. "A deputy or another agent."

"I'll send one of them to look for him."

She shook her head, rejecting his offer. A stranger wouldn't know where to look for Blaine. "You're his friend. You care about him. I trust you and only you to find him and make sure he's okay."

Ash replied, "I am his friend. And that's why he trusted me to protect you."

"You're not protecting me," she said. "I'm not supposed to get upset because of my blood pressure." She had been warned that she had to watch it, that she had to make sure that it didn't stay high. "And not knowing if Blaine is all right is upsetting me."

"Maggie…"

"Please, go find him," she urged his friend. "That's what you can do to protect me." Because not knowing whether or not Blaine had really survived the fire was the greatest risk to her health.

Ash sighed in resignation. "Damn it, if he's okay, he's going to kill me for leaving you. But I'll make sure the man who replaces me on protection duty can be trusted."

She wasn't worried about herself right now. She wasn't even that worried about the baby. The doctors had assured her that he was fine. Now she needed assurance that Blaine was, too.

Just knowing that Ash was looking for him eased her mind some—enough that she eventually drifted off to sleep. And Blaine popped vividly into her mind.

Naked, his golden skin stretched taut over hard muscles. He had made her feel emotions she had never felt before: lust, passion and love.

She hadn't wanted to fall in love with him. But it was too late. She had lost her heart to Special Agent Blaine Campbell. And now she may have lost him.

He should have stayed in the hospital—stayed where they could give him oxygen and monitor him to make sure he had no serious aftereffects from the fire. But he'd gone off on his own to track down killers.

Those zombie-masked men had been dangerous enough when Blaine was in full superhero mode. But in his weakened state, with his injuries...

She shuddered to think of what might have happened to him. But she clung to hope the way she clung to the memories of their lovemaking. With her eyes closed, she relived every kiss, every caress.

Her skin grew hot. But not with passion. She smelled the smoke again and felt the heat of the flames. And in her mind those flames began to consume Blaine...

She jerked awake with a scream on her lips. But a hand covered her mouth, holding that cry inside her. So that she couldn't alert anyone to his presence?

With the lights out, even the bathroom one, she saw only a big, broad-shouldered shadow looming over her. This couldn't be whoever Ash had asked to take his place protecting her. An agent or a deputy—a real one—wouldn't have been standing over her in the dark.

Who was this person?

What were his intentions? To smother her with a pillow? Or simply with his big hand?

She reached up, trying to fight him off. And she smelled the smoke again. This time it wasn't just a vivid memory. This person had been at the fire, too.

Chapter Seventeen

"I'm sorry," Blaine said, his voice gruff from the smoke that still burned in his throat and saturated his hair and clothes. "I didn't mean to scare you." He slid his hand from her lips. But he wanted to cover her mouth again—with his. He wanted to kiss her.

Maggie sat up and threw her arms around his neck. "You did scare me—so badly," she said as she trembled against him. "I thought you didn't make it out of Ash's house."

"Where is Ash?" he asked, furious that his friend hadn't been the one guarding her door. Dalton Reyes had been standing outside, and while Blaine admired what he'd done with the Bureau, he wasn't sure he could trust him, even though Ash obviously did.

"I begged him to look for you," she said.

Begged or manipulated? He shook off the thought, angry with himself for letting Tammy Doremire get to him. She was probably the real manipulator. "Why?" he asked.

"I wanted to make sure that you hadn't had aftereffects from the smoke," she said.

"I'm fine." But he wasn't. He was in even more danger than her almost sister-in-law had warned him about. He was in love with his witness.

"Then where were you all this time?" she asked, her eyes glistening in the darkness as she stared up at him.

Guilt and regret tugged at him for leaving her alone. After the fire, she had to have been terrified. But apparently she'd been more concerned about his safety than hers or she wouldn't have sent her protection away. She wouldn't have sent Ash out to find him.

Anger at Ash flashed through him, but then, he couldn't blame the man for letting her get to him. She had gotten to Blaine, too.

"I was working the case," he said. "Trying to track down a suspect."

"Mark?" she asked. From her tone it was obvious that she was still reluctant to believe Andy's brother could have anything to do with the robberies.

"I went to see Tammy Doremire to see if she'd heard from her husband yet." Mark was definitely one of the robbers—probably the mastermind, no matter that his wife thought he was an idiot.

"Has she heard from him?" she asked with more concern than suspicion.

He shook his head.

"He's her husband," she said. "How can she not know where he is?"

"I don't think their marriage is that great," Blaine said. His sisters would have killed their husbands if they'd gone hours, let alone days, without checking in with them. Hell, Buster probably knew where her husband was every minute of every day.

"Is he seeing someone else?" Maggie wondered.

"Maybe." He was thinking of Susan Iverson, but he added, "She thinks *you* know where he is."

She gasped. "I don't."

"She thinks you two may have been involved." He

could believe that Mark had been interested in Maggie. But he believed that she thought of the man only as an older brother—maybe as a link to her dead fiancé.

She gasped. "That's crazy." And she drew back from him. "Do you think that, too?"

"No." He trusted her. He believed her.

But then he worried that maybe he was being a fool. Maybe she had manipulated him just as Tammy had warned. Maybe Maggie had manipulated Blaine into falling in love with her. Or maybe he was just scared that for the first time in his life he'd fallen in love and he worried that she would never be able to fully love him back. Not when her heart still belonged to her dead fiancé.

BLAINE WAS STANDING there right in front of her, right beside her hospital bed, but Maggie felt him pulling away from her. Whatever Tammy had said must have gotten to him—must have gotten him doubting her.

She felt like a suspect again.

"If I knew where he was, I would tell you," she said. Not because she thought Mark was guilty of anything, but to prove his innocence. Then Blaine would be able to focus on who was really involved in the robberies.

"His wife thinks you know…"

"His wife is paranoid," she said. Tammy had never been nice to her; she was the kind of woman who couldn't be friends with other women. "She's delusional, too, if she thinks I'm having an affair with her husband."

"Maybe there's another reason you might know where Mark is," Blaine said. "Maybe he's hiding someplace that Andy might have gone. Did he have an apartment or a house of his own?"

Everything kept coming back to Andy and those damn

letters she'd written him. If only she'd had something to tell him about other than her job.

If only she'd had the guts to tell him about her feelings, her true feelings…

She shook her head. "No, it would have been crazy for him to have a house or apartment when he was hardly ever home. Andy stayed with his parents whenever he was home on leave—which hadn't been that often since he joined the Marines after high school."

"He wasn't home much?"

After seeing how mean a drunk his father was, she understood why he hadn't come home a lot. "No."

Then she remembered that he hadn't always come home. "He did sometimes stay somewhere else…" She should have thought of it earlier, but it was a place she'd wanted to forget.

That muscle twitched in Blaine's soot-streaked cheek. "Your place?"

"No." As much as she had missed her best friend when he'd been gone so long, she hadn't wanted him to stay with her. She hadn't wanted him to think they were more than they were. She should have said no when he asked her to marry him; she should have refused that ring.

"Then where else had he stayed?" Blaine asked.

"The Doremires have a cabin near Lake Michigan— at least, they had it before Andy died," she said. "I'm not sure if they kept it after they divorced. I can call Mrs. Doremire and ask…"

He shook his head. "No. Let me check it out. I don't want anyone tipping off Mark before I can track him down."

"I'm not so sure his mother would call him." Especially since she hadn't seemed to want anything to do with her life before Andy's death.

Janet Doremire was right—that life was too short to waste. The fire had proved that to Maggie. She was lucky that she hadn't lost her baby and Blaine.

"I don't want to take that risk. Where is the cabin?" he asked.

"It's north of where they live," she said. "Close to Pentwater. But I don't know the name of the actual road. I would need to show you where it is."

He shook his head. "I can't take you along with me. I'll be able to find it. I know that area."

"But you sound like you're from out East," she said.

"New Hampshire," he said. "But my sister lives near Pentwater."

"Which sister?"

"Buster."

She wanted to meet all of his sisters, but most of all Buster because he talked about her with the most affection and exasperation.

"It's good you have family within a four-hour drive." Her family was too far away to offer much support. "So maybe you will stay here even after you find these robbers?"

He shrugged. "I can't think about that until I finish up this case."

Probably because he would be moving on to the next case.

"I need to find that cabin," he said.

"It's really remote and hard to find," she warned him. Even if she could talk Blaine into taking her along, she wasn't certain that she would be able to find the cabin again. She had gone there only a couple of times with Andy—one summer during high school and most recently when he had proposed to her. She shouldn't have gone then. She should have known what he was going to ask her.

"It sounds like the perfect place to hide," Blaine murmured. "He has to be there."

Maybe he was. "But just finding Mark won't prove him guilty of the robberies."

"I'm hoping to find more than Mark. I'm hoping to find the guns, the cash. Hell, if it's so remote, it might be their hideout."

And that meant that he might find not just Mark there, but the other robbers—if Mark really was involved.

"You can't go alone," she warned him. "Not if there's any chance that it's their hideout…"

Because they weren't going to want to be found. Blaine hadn't died in the fire, but that didn't mean that he was safe—especially since he kept willingly risking his life.

BLAINE COULDN'T TAKE her along for so many reasons, but he missed Maggie when she wasn't with him. He worried about her. The doctors had assured them that she was fine. They had even released her.

In his opinion, that had been too soon. But then, keeping her in the hospital wouldn't have ensured her safety. Someone had nearly abducted her from an ER. Had nearly burned her up in the home of an FBI agent.

Maggie wasn't safe anywhere.

Hell, he couldn't even trust her safety to a friend like Ash. She'd gotten to him. So he'd left her in the protection of the one person he knew who could not be sweet-talked or manipulated.

Maggie would be safe.

But as his SUV bounced over the ruts of the two-lane road leading to the cabin, he wondered about his own safety. The place wasn't just remote. It was isolated. He had seen nothing but trees for a long while. This was the kind of place where serial killers would bring their victims, so nobody could hear their screams for help.

Blaine shuddered with foreboding. But maybe he was just overreacting, as Maggie kept insisting. Maybe Mark wasn't involved. Maybe he was just taking a time-out from his jealous wife and his drunken father and the loss of his brother...

Maybe the guy really had nothing to do with the robberies, and Dalton Reyes's informant had identified the wrong guy. As Maggie had pointed out, a lot of guys looked like Mark Doremire. Andy had. Hell, even Ash did.

Even though he would have to start all over looking for suspects, Blaine almost hoped Mark had nothing to do with the robberies. If he didn't, Blaine could just check in with him and make sure that everything was all right with the man.

Then he could return to Maggie and ease her worries about her letters to Andy inspiring the robberies. She already took on too much responsibility for everything that had happened. Maybe that was his fault, too—for being so suspicious of her. Maybe he should have told her that he trusted her.

Instead he had pulled away from her. Physically and emotionally. He needed distance. He needed perspective. Hell, maybe if Mark wasn't at the cabin, Blaine would hang out for a while. He would try to regain his lost perspective.

But he worried that time and distance wouldn't change his feelings for Maggie. He would probably always love her. And she would probably always love Andy.

Finally some of the trees gave way on one side of the two-track road, making a small space for a little log cabin. Blaine couldn't see any vehicles. Only a small space of the dense woods had been cleared for the cabin, so he doubted there were any vehicles parked around the back.

Maybe Maggie had been right. Mark wasn't here. Coming here had probably been a waste of Blaine's time. Because no matter how much distance he gained, he was unlikely to gain any new insights.

Still, he shut off the SUV and stepped out of it. He would take some more time to enjoy the silence.

To clear his head.

But the silence shattered as gunfire erupted. And Blaine worried that he was more likely to lose his head than clear it.

Chapter Eighteen

Maggie had wanted to meet Buster, but not like this—not riding along in the Michigan state trooper's police cruiser. At least Buster had let her ride in the passenger's seat and not the back.

The woman had pulled off into a parking lot, and now she studied Maggie through narrowed eyes that were the same bright green as her brother's. She was blonde, too, but most of her hair was tucked up under a brown, broad-brimmed trooper hat, so it wasn't possible to tell if it was golden, like his, or lighter.

She was older than he was but not more than a few years. And she was even less approachable. Maggie, who usually had no problem making conversation, had no idea what to say to the woman, so an awkward silence had fallen between them—broken only by an occasional squawk of the police radio.

Finally Buster cleared her throat and remarked, "Blaine has never asked me to guard anybody for him."

"I'm sorry for being such an inconvenience," Maggie said. "I know you're too busy for babysitting."

"I have four hyper kids and an idiot husband," Buster shared, "so I'm used to babysitting."

The heat of embarrassment rushed to Maggie's face. She hated feeling so helpless and dependent.

But then Buster continued, "*This* isn't babysitting. Nobody is trying to kill my kids or my husband—except for me when they piss me off too much. You're in real danger."

Maggie felt safe, though, with Blaine's older sister. She had an authority about her—the same authority that had Blaine easily taking over the bank investigation and her protection duty.

"Blaine is the one in danger now," Maggie said, as nerves fluttered in her belly with the baby's kicks. "He's trying so hard to track down those robbers."

"That's his job," Buster said. "He's been doing it for a while. And he's been doing it well."

Maybe he was right about Mark, then. Maggie hadn't wanted to believe Andy's brother capable of violence, but she was on edge and it had less to do with how Buster was studying her and more to do with the danger she felt Blaine was facing. "I'm still worried about him."

"I see that…"

With the way she had been staring at Maggie, she had probably seen a lot. More than Maggie was comfortable with her seeing.

Buster continued, "I see that you love him."

Maggie's breath shuddered out in a ragged sigh. She could have lied—although she sucked at it—and said Buster was mistaken. But she wasn't a liar. And maybe it would relieve some of the pressure on her chest—and her heart—if she admitted to her feelings. "Yes…"

"You could have denied it," Buster said.

"Why?"

"Because you haven't told him yet," his sister replied. "And he's the one you should have told first."

Maggie shook her head. "I can't tell him at all." Ever.

"Why not?"

"Because he doesn't have the same feelings for me that I do for him," Maggie said. "And I would just embarrass him." The way she had at the hospital when she'd clung to him, refusing to let him leave without her.

"Blaine doesn't embarrass easily," Buster said. "Trust me. I've tried." She chuckled. "He has three older sisters. He may not get embarrassed at all anymore."

Maggie laughed, too, as she imagined a young Blaine enduring his siblings' teasing and tormenting. He had probably handled it as stoically then as he handled everything now. Her laughter faded. "It may not embarrass him, but it would make it awkward for him. He's only doing his job—"

"He has never asked me to protect anyone for him before," Buster repeated as if that was monumental.

As if it meant something.

Could he return her feelings?

Maggie shook her head. "That's because I'm in a lot of danger," she said. "People have been trying to kidnap and kill me."

"People?"

"He thinks the brother of my..." She didn't know what to call Andy. While she had accepted his proposal, she'd done it only to avoid hurting him, not because she'd ever intended to actually marry him.

"Baby daddy?" Buster supplied the title for her.

Maggie laughed again. But Andy would have been appalled at that title, especially since he'd been trying so long to get her to marry him. He'd wanted to marry right out of high school, but she'd told him she wanted to go to college first. And then when she'd graduated, he had suggested they get married. But she'd put him off, saying that she wanted to get her career established first.

Poor Andy...

Buster reached across the console and squeezed her hand. "You cared about him."

"We were friends since sixth grade, when my family and I moved to town. He was the first person who was nice to the new girl in class." Because he had been nice to her, she had latched on to him, declaring them best friends. But Andy hadn't wanted to be just a friend.

Buster nodded as if Maggie's words had given her sudden understanding. "So he's the only boy you ever dated?"

"Yes," Maggie replied.

"It must have been hard losing him and finding yourself alone," Buster said, "with a baby on the way."

Did Buster think that Maggie was afraid to be alone? That that was why she'd fallen in love with Blaine? Because he'd been nice to her? Maggie knew that he was only doing his job, though. He didn't want more than friendship from her; he probably didn't even want friendship.

"But that's not why I..." she began defensively, "...why I have feelings for your brother." She couldn't say it—couldn't express those feelings.

"That's not why you've fallen for my brother," Buster said, as if she didn't doubt her.

"He might not believe that, though," Maggie said. "Or he might think I'm just grateful for all the times he has saved my life and the baby's."

"May I?" Buster asked, as she moved her hand from Maggie's arm to her stomach. She smiled as the baby kicked beneath her palm. "You should tell Blaine how you feel about him. That's the only way you're going to know what he thinks and how he feels about you."

Was it possible that he could return her feelings? He had made love with her. He'd wanted her...

"My brother has never been an easy man to read," Buster said. "Hell, he wasn't even easy to read when he was a little boy. It's always been hard to tell what Blaine is thinking or feeling. So don't assume that you know."

Maggie had been making assumptions. But it wasn't based so much on what she thought of Blaine but more on what she thought of herself. She didn't believe that she, especially pregnant, could ever attract a man like Blaine Campbell. The gorgeous FBI special agent was more of a superhero than a regular man. "But—"

"Do you want any more regrets?" Buster interrupted. "It seems like you already have a few."

About Andy. About never telling him the truth...

"I don't regret my baby," Maggie said, anger rushing over her.

"I know," Buster said. "And I am a firm believer in everything happening for a reason. So stop beating yourself up about the baby's daddy."

Apparently Maggie wasn't very hard to read at all.

Buster patted Maggie's belly. "Remember—everything happens for a reason."

Because she carried his child, Maggie would always have a piece of Andy with her. She hadn't completely lost her best friend.

"You're right," Maggie agreed.

But she didn't have a chance to tell Buster exactly what she was right about because the police radio squawked again—interrupting them. "Shots fired during FBI raid on cabin. Possible casualties..."

She grabbed Buster's hand and clutched it. Possible casualties? Was one of them Blaine? Had he been shot?

"WE DIDN'T FIND the shooters," Trooper Littlefield reported to Blaine. He was one of Buster's coworkers.

He had provided backup—along with a couple of FBI agents—in case the cabin had been the robbers' hide-out. But they had arrived early and hidden in the woods so that it would look as though Blaine had come alone.

Blaine had even felt alone in the middle of the woods. These law-enforcement officers were so good that he hadn't seen a single one of them—until the gunfire had erupted. Then they'd stepped out of their hiding spots and returned fire—giving him cover so that none of the shots had actually struck him.

"They had a vehicle parked on a two-track gravel road that led to another cabin, and before we could block them in, they'd gotten away," the trooper said regretfully.

Blaine sighed. They had eluded him so many times that he wasn't surprised. "In a van?"

The trooper nodded.

Dalton Reyes stepped up to him. "Another stolen one," he confirmed with a curse. "The guy who ordered this one isn't the one that my informant ID'd, though. She claims she hasn't seen him again."

Blaine had a bad feeling that Mark Doremire was already gone. But still he held out hope. "You sure you can trust your informant?" he asked. Mark was a flirt; maybe he'd turned the woman to his side.

"I don't really trust anyone." Reyes shrugged. "Maybe she's been lying to me."

"Do you think any of the guys you're after could be involved in the robberies?" Blaine asked. "There were five guys at the bank." But more could have been involved.

He had no idea how many had been shooting at him in the woods.

Dalton shrugged again. "I'm not sure. I didn't get a look at any of the shooters."

"And the guy inside the cabin?" Blaine asked, as he

walked back into the run-down log structure. He'd already been inside but Agent Reyes hadn't. He hoped Dalton recognized the corpse because Blaine was afraid that he did.

Dalton checked out the scene and cursed. The guy was slumped over in a wooden chair, a pool of blood dried beneath him. His clothes—a camo shirt and pants—were also saturated and hard with dried blood. Bloody bandages were strewn across the table in front of him.

But those weren't the only things on the table. A pile of envelopes, bound with a big rubber band, sat atop the scarred wooden surface, too.

Maggie's letters…written to her fiancé. Blaine hadn't looked at them; he probably wouldn't be able to look at them. But he knew they were hers.

"What the hell happened to him?" Dalton asked.

"I think I killed him."

Dalton snorted. "This guy has been dead for days. You didn't do this."

"I think I did. During the bank robbery," he said. "That first van that was recovered had blood inside, and I did get off some shots during the robbery."

Ash stepped into the cabin behind Dalton. "Is he the one?"

Blaine nodded. "Yeah, I'm pretty sure this is the guy who shot Sarge."

Ash patted his shoulder. "You got him!"

"I wasn't sure I hit him. They were wearing vests…"

This guy's vest was lying on the floor near his chair along with the zombie mask and the trench coat. He had definitely been one of the robbers. Was he the one who'd killed Sarge?

When Blaine had fired back, he'd thought that he shot the one who'd hit Sarge.

"He must not have had his vest tight on the sides," Dalton said as he leaned over to inspect it. "Looks like it was too small for him—probably left a gap."

So Blaine had gotten a lucky shot into the guy's side. "There was a smaller robber—maybe their vests got mixed up…"

"I don't care what happened," Ash said. "I just care that you got him—for Sarge."

But who was he? Blaine stepped closer to the body, intent on tipping back the guy's head to get a better look. But then a glint of metal caught his eye, and he saw the dog tags dangling from the chain around the corpse's neck.

He picked up the tags and read, "'Sergeant Andrew Doremire…'"

"Who the hell is that?" Ash asked.

"A dead man," Blaine replied. He tipped up the face— he looked like the man on the security footage from the bank. Maggie had said that Andy and Mark looked eerily similar.

Dalton snorted. "Obviously…"

"No, he's Maggie's dead fiancé."

Dalton Reyes cursed. "Do you think she knows he didn't really die in Afghanistan?" Of course he would ask that; he'd already said he didn't trust anyone.

"No way," Blaine said with absolute certainty. Maggie carried too much guilt over his death, probably because she hadn't been able to talk him out of joining the Marines. But she hadn't been to blame for Andy's death.

Blaine was.

Apparently Dustin Doremire hadn't just been a delusional drunk. He'd been right. Andy wasn't dead—or, at least, he hadn't been until Blaine had shot him.

"He was one of Sarge's drills," Ash said. "He must

have been worried that Sarge had recognized him. That's why he killed him."

Or because Sarge had been trying to kill *him*...

Blaine pushed a hand through his hair. "That must have been why they were trying to take Maggie along with them—they probably thought she recognized him, too."

But she hadn't. She had refused to accept that even the brother of her childhood sweetheart could have had anything to do with criminal activities. She would never believe that Andy had.

So who were the other robbers? Definitely Andy's brother—unless the informant had mistaken Mark's picture for his younger brother. But if his brother hadn't been involved, where the hell was he?

Maybe even Andy's father was involved. That could have been why he'd been drinking so heavily when they'd gone to see him—because he'd known that Andy wasn't going to survive this time.

Blaine had killed him. Would Maggie be able to forgive him? Would she be able to forgive herself?

Chapter Nineteen

He was alive!

Blaine was alive.

Her heart leaped for joy the moment she saw him walk through the door of his sister's sprawling ranch house. When he'd asked Buster to protect her, he hadn't wanted her to take Maggie to her home—he hadn't wanted her to put her family at risk. Neither had Maggie.

But when they had been waiting to hear about Blaine, Buster had insisted on bringing Maggie home with her. In case the news was bad, Buster had probably wanted to be close to her family.

Her kids had gathered around them. She had three boys and one little girl—the opposite of Buster and her siblings. The boys had lost interest in Maggie quickly and gone back to playing with trucks in the living room while Maggie and Buster waited in the big country kitchen. Although shy, the little blonde girl had crept close to Maggie and pressed pudgy little fingers against her belly.

"Baby?" she had asked, though she was little more than a baby herself.

"Yes," Maggie had replied. And she had even managed a laugh when the baby kicked and the little girl had jumped away in surprise.

But fear for Blaine's safety had pressed heavily on

Maggie until he walked through the door. His bruises and scrapes were from the night before—from the fire. Otherwise he was unscathed from the shooting. Maggie had never been happier to see anyone in her life.

But she didn't dare launch herself into his arms the way she wanted to. He had that wall around him—that wall he'd put up back at the hospital. Something was wrong. Maybe it was just that he'd realized he had lost perspective with her, and he was trying to be more professional.

Buster pulled Blaine into a tight hug. "Thank God, you're all right. We were going crazy worrying about you."

"Why?"

"We heard the call on the radio," Buster said, "about the shooting and a possible casualty."

The little girl tugged on her mama's leg. "What's a castle tea?"

Buster pulled back from her brother and picked up her daughter. "It's nothing…"

But it wasn't. Maggie saw the look of regret on Blaine's face. Then he leaned forward and kissed his niece's cheek. "Hey, beautiful girl…"

"Hey, Unca Bane…"

Buster chuckled.

The boys abandoned their trucks and rushed into the kitchen, launching themselves at Blaine the way Maggie wished she had. She wanted his arms around her like they were around his nephews and niece.

"They're so many of you," he murmured. "You have your own Brady Bunch, Buster."

"There are only four—five counting Carl," she said. "But he had to go to work."

"Is that why you came home?"

She bit her lip and shook her head.

"It's because of what you heard on the radio?" He glanced at his niece. "About the castle tea?"

Buster nodded.

"I'm fine," he said. "I had no idea you would have heard…" He stopped himself. "That's right—there was a trooper along for backup."

"Since you're fine, us troopers must be good for something, huh, Mr. Special Agent?" Her green eyes twinkled as she teased him.

He shrugged. "I had a couple other special agents along," he said. "That's why I'm fine."

She gently punched his shoulder. Then she turned to where Maggie sat on the kitchen chair, watching them and wishing she was part of their loving family. Buster must have seen that longing because she reached out for Maggie's hand and tugged her up from the chair. Buster sighed and remarked, "You are so beautiful pregnant. If I'd looked like you, instead of a beached whale, I might have had a couple more."

"God help us," Blaine muttered.

He already had as far as Maggie was concerned, since he'd brought Blaine safely back to his family. And her…

But he wasn't hers. He had yet to even look at her. Maybe he was mad that she was at his sister's home— endangering his sister's beautiful family.

"I'm sorry," she said. "I know you didn't want me here. We can leave now."

Buster stared at her with wide eyes, urging her to tell Blaine her feelings. But Maggie shook her head. It was obvious to her that he didn't want her love. Why couldn't his sister see the emotional distance he'd put between himself and Maggie?

"We'll leave in a little while," he said, finally speaking

directly to her. But still, he wouldn't look at her. Instead he turned back to Buster. "Can we have a few minutes alone? Maybe in the sunroom?"

Buster nodded. "Of course."

He took Maggie's arm and drew her from the kitchen through a set of French doors off the family room. He pulled the doors closed behind him, shutting them alone in a solarium of windows. But the sun had already dropped, so the room was growing dark and cold.

Maggie shivered.

"If you're cold—"

"No, I'm fine," she said. "Why do you want to talk to me privately?" Did he want to yell at her for endangering his family? "I told Buster it was a bad idea to bring me back here."

"Buster rarely listens to anyone but herself," he replied. "Poor Carl…"

She suspected that Carl was a very lucky man, and that he was smart enough to know it. No matter how much she joked about her husband, it was obvious that Buster loved him very much.

The way Maggie loved Blaine…

"Why did you want me alone?" she asked again. She tamped down the hope that threatened to burgeon—the hope that he wanted to tell her his feelings.

But that hope deflated when he finally replied, "I have to show you something."

Instinctively she knew it wasn't something she would want to see. He didn't even *want* to show it to her. He *had* to…and even without his choice of words, she would have picked up on his reluctance from the gruffness of his voice.

"Did you find the letters?" she asked. If they'd been at the cabin and if it had been used as a hideout, then the robberies were her fault. She shouldn't have talked so much about the bank. Her mother was right; she had always talked too much. Even though she hadn't given out security passwords or anything, she'd talked too much about her duties as the assistant manager. And it wasn't as if Andy had actually been interested; she'd just rambled.

"Yes, I found your letters," he replied. But he didn't hold them out for her to look at; he held out a photograph instead.

She didn't look at it. First she had to know, "What's this?"

"You tell me," he said as he lifted it toward her face. "Is it Andy?"

Her heart leaped again. Was it possible that Andy was alive? But then she looked at the picture. The man in it wasn't alive. And he wasn't Andy, either.

"Why would you think that was Andy?" She'd thought he had realized that Mr. Doremire had been drunk and delusional when he'd made those wild claims about Andy faking his death and the Marines covering it up.

"He had on Andy's dog tags."

The dog tags that his father claimed had never been found. No wonder Blaine had thought it was Andy. She shook her head.

"He must have been mistaken," she said. And with as much as he drank, it would be understandable.

"The dog tags must have been in his personal effects along with the letters," she explained. "His brother must have taken them when he took the letters."

"Now you think Mark took the dog tags?" he asked.

She pointed at the photo. "That's Mark, so he must have, since he was wearing them when he died."

"You're sure that's Mark?"

"I'm sure," she said. "I'm surprised you didn't recognize him from the security footage." But he did look different dead. He didn't look like the smiling man on the television monitor.

Blaine released a ragged breath as if he had been holding it for a while, maybe since he'd found the body and had thought it was Andy. "I think he's the robber I shot at the bank."

Shock and regret had her gasping. She remembered that horrific moment—remembered Blaine firing back at the man who'd shot the security guard. "You think he's the one who killed Sarge?"

Mark had been like her big brother, too. He had always seemed as sweet and easygoing as Andy had been, and he had adored his younger brother. How could he have killed a man that Andy had loved? A man she had loved, as well?

Sarge had been so kind and supportive after Andy's death. He had kept checking on her. Maybe he had made a promise to Andy. Mark must not have. Or, if he had, it was a promise he'd broken.

Blaine nodded. "He was wearing a vest that was too small for him. I got a shot into his side. He bled out from the wound."

"Nobody got him help?" she asked, horrified that his coconspirators would have just let him bleed to death.

Blaine shook his head. "No. They got him to the cabin, but they couldn't stop the bleeding."

"He wasn't the one who tried grabbing me at the hospital, then," she said. "That man was healthy and strong." It gave her some relief that Mark hadn't been trying to hurt her. "He couldn't have been behind any of those other attempts on our lives."

"No," Blaine agreed. "It must've been whoever he was working with."

There had been five of them. So four other men were still out there, apparently still determined to kill her and Special Agent Blaine Campbell.

BLAINE HUSTLED HER quickly out of his sister's house. It was less for his family's safety and more for hers. He wanted to protect her. He also wanted to comfort her because he had seen the fear on her face when she'd realized that she was still in danger.

"We'll be safe here," he said, as he locked the motel room door behind them. He could have driven her back to Chicago. But night had already fallen, and she was obviously exhausted. She trembled with it and maybe with cold. He turned up the thermostat as she shivered.

"I thought you weren't going to protect me anymore," she said. "Didn't your boss tell you that you shouldn't?"

He nodded. "And he's right."

"You said that last night…"

Before he had made love to her. What the hell had he been thinking to take advantage of her that way?

"I'm sorry," he said. "About last night…"

"You didn't start the fire," she said.

"But I should have been awake. I should have been alert," he said. "My boss was right. You will be safer with someone else protecting you."

"I feel safe with you," she said, and she turned back to him and stared up at him with those chocolaty brown eyes.

There was such an overall glow about her. Maybe it was the pregnancy. But he suspected it was just her— just Maggie's warm personality. She had even won over Buster and that was never easy to do.

"Maggie, I have to focus on the case," he said. He hoped she would understand that he couldn't let her distract him any longer. "I have to dig deeper into Mark's life and find all of his associates."

"I can help you," she said.

"You know his friends?"

She shook her head. "He was older than me and Andy, so I don't know who he hung out with." She nibbled her lower lip. "I guess I can't help you."

"You need to focus on yourself and your baby," he said. "Stay healthy. Stay well."

She touched her belly with trembling hands. "Yes…"

"I will find them all," Blaine promised. "I'll stop them." He just hoped he could stop them before they tried to kill her again. They obviously cared little for human life since they had let one of their own die instead of getting him help. To save themselves…

So, even dead, Mark could lead him to the others. That must have been the reason they hadn't sought out medical attention or wanted his body found.

"Thank you," she said.

"I haven't done anything yet," he said.

"You've saved my life," she reminded him. "Many times. Thank you for that."

He shrugged off her gratitude. "I was just doing my job." But it was so much more than that, and they both knew it.

"And thank you for last night," she said, "for making me feel desirable. Wanted…"

He wanted her again. But he kept his hands at his sides. He wouldn't reach for her again.

But she reached for him. Sliding her arms around him, she pressed her voluptuous body close to his. And the tenuous hold he'd had on his control snapped. He couldn't resist her sweetness, her passion.

She rose up on tiptoe and pressed her lips to his, sliding them across his mouth—arousing his desire. He kissed her back.

She eased away from him but only to ease her hands between them and undo the buttons of his shirt. He helped her take off his holster. And his jeans…

She gasped, as she so often did, as she stared at his nakedness. "You are the most beautiful man."

Maggie's words filled him with heat and pride.

She touched him, her fingers caressing his skin. "You were hurt last night."

He had some scrapes, a couple of first-degree burns. "It's nothing."

She shuddered. "When that roof caved in, I thought you were gone. And then when we heard that radio call…"

"About the castle tea?" he teased.

But she didn't laugh. In fact, her eyes glistened with tears. "I was so scared."

He drew her against him and held her close. "I hate that you were scared."

But he was scared, too. He was scared that he'd irrevocably fallen for her.

"Make me forget my fears," she challenged him. "Make me forget about everything but you. Make love to me…"

He couldn't refuse her wishes. He helped her off with her clothes and then helped her into bed. Joining her, he kissed and stroked every inch of her silky skin. And with every kiss and every caress, she gasped or moaned and squirmed beneath him. Then she caressed him back, running her soft hands over his back and his hips and lower. She encircled him with those hands. He nearly lost his mind, but he fought for control. He wanted to give her pleasure.

So he made love to her with his mouth. She cried out. But this was a cry he loved to hear from her—a cry of pleasure as she found release. Then, carefully, he joined their bodies. He tried to move slowly and gently.

But she arched and thrust up her hips. And her inner muscles clenched around him, tugging him deeper inside until he didn't know where she ended and he began. They were one. And as one, they reached ecstasy—shouting each other's name.

He held her close as they both panted for breath. He held her and waited—for the next attempt on their lives. He didn't know if it would be another fire or more shooting. He didn't know what it would be; he just knew that it would happen. As if on some level he had known that he would fall for Maggie Jenkins.

She had taken his heart. Now he just had to hold on to his life…

Chapter Twenty

Maybe it had been only days. But it felt like weeks since Maggie had last seen Blaine. She knew he was busy working the case. He had explained that he had to hand off her protection to someone else so that he could focus.

Had she distracted him?

She was working again, too. But she was preoccupied by thoughts of Blaine. It wouldn't matter how long she went without seeing him; she knew she would never *not* think of Special Agent Blaine Campbell.

A noise at her office door startled her, and she jumped.

"Sorry," the bank manager said. "I didn't mean to frighten you."

"It's not your fault," she assured him. Even though no attempts had been made to kidnap or kill her the past few days, she was still on edge. Still waiting for the robbers in their hideous masks to burst through the bank doors or into her apartment with their guns drawn.

"Has everything been all right?" he asked.

She nodded instead of uttering a lie. Because everything was not all right—not without Blaine. She ached for him.

"Things are back to normal now," Mr. Hardy said with a sigh of relief as he gazed around at the bank. The glass had all been repaired. Everything was back in its place as if the robbery had never happened. "And with one of the robbers found dead, maybe the others have gone into hiding."

"Agent Campbell will catch them," she said with unshakable confidence.

"Hopefully," he said, but he sounded doubtful. "I understand that the robber that was found dead was related to you."

"No," she said.

"Well," he said again, his voice rising with a slight whine, "he would've been had your fiancé not died."

She wouldn't have married Andy, though—even after finding out she carried his child. She hadn't wanted friendship love in her marriage; she'd wanted passionate love. She had wanted to be in love, not just to love someone. She had finally found that with Blaine, but he didn't want the instant family he would have with her. He probably didn't even want a relationship. He was totally focused on his career—so much so that she hadn't even heard from him.

Mr. Hardy was looking at her strangely. Then Maggie recognized the suspicion. "I was not involved in the robberies," she said. "I had nothing to do with them."

Except for those damn letters she'd written. Did he know about those, too?

He nodded. "Of course you didn't..."

But she heard the doubt in his voice. "I need this job, Mr. Hardy. I wouldn't have done anything to jeopardize it."

"Susan Iverson thinks you may have been involved with that man."

"Susan may have been," Maggie said. "But I wasn't. He's just someone I used to know." And apparently she hadn't known him nearly as well as she'd thought she had. "Like Susan, he proved to be someone I couldn't trust."

"She claims that the agent totally misread the situation when he found her in your apartment—"

"Stealing my engagement ring," she said.

"She assured me she wasn't stealing it," he defended the blonde bank teller. "That she was only looking for evidence that you were involved in the robberies."

Maggie shook her head. She'd had enough of people lying and scamming her. "She used my credit cards," she said. "She can't explain that away."

"You owed her rent money."

Anger surged through her, and she stood up. "That's a lie. And if you choose to believe her lies over me, maybe I don't need this job as much as I thought."

He held out his hands. "Calm down, Maggie. I know this is an emotional time for you. Susan needs her job, too, and if you drop the charges against her, I think you could work together again."

Blaine had caught the woman in the act of stealing. It wasn't up to Maggie whether or not charges were pressed. But she didn't bother explaining that.

"Why are you defending her?" she wondered. And then, as color flooded his face, she realized why. He was involved with the young teller. "Oh…"

"I don't know what you're thinking," he said fearfully, as if he actually did know, "but you're wrong."

"No, *you're* wrong." Especially if he had betrayed his wife with the blonde opportunist. "There actually is evidence against her, and she will be prosecuted. I couldn't drop the charges even if I wanted to."

Maybe Susan had been involved in the robberies, too. Maggie wouldn't put anything past the woman. She was a user. Mr. Hardy would figure that out soon enough.

Disgusted with him, she grabbed her purse and said, "I'm going home."

"Yes, get some rest and think about it," he suggested.

Maybe Maggie needed to return to the branch where she had previously worked. She couldn't work for Mr. Hardy anymore. She couldn't work with Susan Iverson. Maybe she needed to join her parents in Hong Kong. It wasn't as if Blaine would miss her. He had gone days with no contact.

As she headed out the door, her new protector followed her. The burly young man, Truman Jackson, was something with the Bureau—maybe a new recruit. Since there had been no recent attempts to grab her, she doubted they would have wasted a special agent on babysitting duty. She had been lucky to have Blaine as long as she had.

"Are you all right, Miss Jenkins?" the young man asked as he helped her into his unmarked vehicle.

"Maggie," she corrected him as she had the past few days. "And I'm fine."

"But you're leaving early…"

She hadn't done that the past couple of days. In fact, she had worked late, trying to catch up from the time the bank had been closed for repairs.

"I'm tired," she said. And that was no lie. She was exhausted. From looking over her shoulder. From worrying. From missing Blaine.

"So you want to go right back to your apartment?" Truman asked.

"Yes, please," she said, and happy that he was driving, she closed her eyes and relaxed as much as she could.

"Do you think I'll need protection much longer?" she asked. If no more attempts were made on her life…

"I couldn't say, Maggie."

"Do you know if Special Agent Campbell has gotten any closer to apprehending the other bank robbers?" She wanted to know what was going on with the case, but most of all she wanted to know what was going on with Blaine.

Was he okay? Had he recovered completely from the fire? Had anyone tried to kill him again?

Truman shrugged his broad shoulders; one of them nudged hers. "I don't know," he replied. "Do you have his number? Could you call and ask?"

No. She hadn't been given his number. He had barely looked at her as he'd passed off her protection to someone else.

"I don't want to bother him," she said. And that was true. She didn't want to distract him anymore. He had a job to do, and she had only been part of that job to him.

Truman had lost interest in their conversation, his attention on her apartment door as he pulled into the parking lot. He reached for his holster. "Who is that?"

A woman stood outside the door. She wore dark glasses that obscured most of her face, but Maggie recognized the bright glow of her red hair.

"It's my…" almost sister-in-law? "…friend." But Tammy had never really been her friend—not even when they were younger. Like Maggie and Andy, Tammy and Mark had dated all during high school. Tammy had actually been there when Mark had sneaked her and Andy into that horror movie. She had thought Maggie's fear funny—as Mark had. And recently Tammy had been suspicious and resentful of Maggie. She had even suspected her of cheating with Mark.

Was that why she'd come here? To lash out some more in her grief? Maggie wasn't certain how much more she could take today.

BLAINE GRABBED AT his tie, struggling to loosen the knot. He felt suffocated within the walls of his new office, and he felt buried beneath the files atop his new desk. He would rather be out in the field, physically tracking down solid leads instead of fumbling through piles of paper.

He would actually rather be with Maggie, making certain that she was safe. There had been no new attempts on her life. But he was not a fool enough to think that it was over, not with so many of Mark's associates out there yet. Blaine was only a fool for Maggie—for falling for her.

As he'd had to so many times over the past few days, he pushed thoughts of Maggie from his mind and focused on the case again. He grabbed a file from the stack and read over the names of Mark Doremire's friends and family. Was old man Doremire one of the robbers?

Hell, was Andy? Maybe the guy wasn't really dead.

Blaine shook his head. He was losing it. Andy was gone. But another name on his list looked familiar. He shuffled through the other folders for the report from the security chief at the hospital, and he pulled out her list of employees. One of the names matched.

Mark Doremire's brother-in-law worked security at the hospital. Hadn't Tammy Doremire told him she had no friends or family in the area? Why had she lied to Blaine?

Had she been trying to protect her brother since she must already have known that she'd lost her husband? If her brother had been in on the thefts, she would have known that Mark had been hurt.

Maybe she had even been along for the robberies. Blaine touched his tablet and played some of the security footage from the holdup. There had been a robber who was smaller than the others. It was the one who'd dragged Maggie to the back door of the bank, the one who'd pulled her into the van.

Tammy Doremire wasn't just related to a couple of the robbers. She was one of them.

He just had to find the other two. They might be associates of her brother's. Or...

His phone rang, drawing his attention from all those files. He clicked the talk button. "Campbell."

"Special Agent Campbell?"

"Yes."

"This is Truman Jackson," a male voice said.

"You're the guard on Maggie." Blaine's heart slammed against his ribs as fear overwhelmed him. Before letting Truman protect her again, he had made certain that the man had not been compromised—that he could be trusted. Ash Stryker had vouched for him, so Truman had been chosen as her new protector. Had he failed his duty?

"Is she okay?" Blaine anxiously asked. "Has there been another attempt on her life?"

"No, no," the man quickly assured Blaine. But there was concern in his voice.

That concern had Blaine grabbing his keys and rushing out of his office. But even outside the confining walls, he couldn't breathe. Now panic and concern suffocated him.

"What's going on?" he asked. What had compelled the man to call him?

"I brought Maggie home from the bank," Truman relayed, "and there was a woman waiting at her apartment door."

At least she had been at the door and hadn't let herself inside the way Susan Iverson had. But maybe Susan had learned her lesson about doing that.

"Who was she?" Blaine asked.

"Maggie," he said, "told me that the woman was a friend but…"

"But what?"

"I don't know," the man replied. "But I didn't pick up the friendship vibe from her. Maggie insisted on speaking alone with the woman, though, so I left them together in Maggie's apartment."

Blaine clicked the lock on his SUV and jumped behind the wheel. "Did you check the woman for a weapon before you left them alone?"

"Of course," the man replied, as if offended. "She wasn't armed. And she's too thin to do any physical harm to Maggie."

That didn't ease Blaine's fears any. "Who is she?"

"A red-haired woman," Truman replied. "I checked her license."

Blaine didn't even need her name for confirmation. He knew who was with Maggie.

"Tammy Doremire…"

The robber from the bank—the one who had tried bringing Maggie along. Probably the only one who really wanted her dead…

Chapter Twenty-One

Maggie handed Tammy a cup of tea. Brewing it had bought her some time to gather her thoughts since she had no idea what to say to the new widow.

But Tammy must not have wanted the tea because she set the cup on the coffee table in front of her. Maggie kept hers in her hands, hoping the heat of the mug would warm her. But she still shivered—maybe more with nerves than cold.

"You still have a bodyguard," the other woman said.

It hadn't been a question, but Maggie nodded in reply. Truman had searched Tammy to make sure she carried no weapon, so of course she would have realized he was a bodyguard.

"But there haven't been any attempts lately," Tammy said. "It seems like the FBI wouldn't want to waste manpower."

"I don't know," Maggie replied. She had no idea why Tammy cared about the bodyguard or the FBI, let alone how she would have known about the attempts on Maggie's life.

Unless...

No, she refused to suspect the worst of everyone; she refused to be as cynical as Blaine had been. But Blaine had been right about Mark...

"Having protection for you is probably Agent Campbell's idea," the woman continued, her voice sharp with bitterness as she said his name. "I'm surprised that he's not still personally protecting you."

"He's busy," Maggie said. At least that was what she was telling herself to salve her wounded heart.

Tammy sighed. "It doesn't matter."

But it did matter to Maggie that she hadn't heard from Blaine—that she didn't know exactly what he was doing. Or feeling.

Since the mug was beginning to cool, Maggie set it beside Tammy's on the coffee table. But she didn't join her on the couch or settle onto one of the chairs across from her. Maggie didn't feel comfortable enough with this woman to sit down with her.

But she should have gone to see her earlier out of respect. "I'm glad you came over," Maggie said.

"You are?" Tammy asked skeptically.

"Of course. I've been wanting to talk to you, wanting to tell you how sorry I am about Mark." Of course she hadn't known how to express sympathy for a man dying in the commission of a crime—of a murder. If only Mark hadn't been involved in the robberies...

Both he and Sarge would be alive. How could Maggie express sympathy for that?

The woman ignored her remarks and pointed out a box that sat on the end of the coffee table. Wrapping paper with little rubber ducks covered the box, and a bright yellow bow topped it. "What's that?"

"I don't know," Maggie said. She hadn't noticed it earlier. Tammy hadn't had it with her when Truman had searched her body and her purse. He would have found the brightly wrapped package. "It wasn't here this morning."

"Maybe it was delivered today," Tammy suggested.

Maggie shook her head. "Then it would have been left outside the door." Not on her coffee table.

"Maybe your elderly janitor brought it inside for you."

Maggie's skin chilled as she realized that Tammy wasn't offering a possible explanation but a fact. She knew because she had given it to Mr. Simmons to bring inside for her. Why?

"This is yours?" Maggie asked. "You brought this for me?" Despite what she'd told Truman, they weren't friends. Why would the woman have brought her a baby gift?

"Yes," Tammy replied. "But let me open it for you." She tore the ribbon and easily slipped the top off the box. Then she smiled and lifted a gun out. "Now tell me how sorry you are about Mark."

Fear slammed into Maggie as she stared down the barrel of that gun. She covered her belly with her palms—even though she knew there was no way to protect her baby from a bullet. "What are you doing?"

"I'm going to do what we should have done at the first bank so you wouldn't have time to figure out it was us and report us to the FBI," Tammy said. "I'm going to kill you."

"But the guard is just outside the door," Maggie reminded her. "Truman is going to hear the shot. You won't get away with this. He might even shoot you."

"You think I have anything to live for?" Tammy asked, her face contorting into a mask of pain and hatred nearly as grotesque as those zombie masks. Tammy must have chosen them; she had found it funniest that Maggie had been so afraid during that movie. "Mark's dead because of you."

"I didn't shoot him," Maggie said.

"No, your FBI agent shot him," Tammy said. "I had

hoped that he was the one protecting you. That he would be here, so that I could kill you both."

"You've got your wish," a deep voice murmured as the apartment door opened with a slight creak of the hinges. "I'm here."

Maggie had spent the past few days missing Blaine and longing to see his handsome face again. But not now. She would rather have never seen him again than to have him die with her.

BLAINE HAD EXPECTED the gun because he'd met Mr. Simmons at the door. The older gentleman had wanted to make certain that Maggie got the baby gift that he'd put in her apartment for the red-haired woman. He'd thought the box was heavy for a baby-shower gift.

Of course it held no gift for Maggie or her baby. It had held the gun.

Tammy was clever—so clever that she had probably been the one who had actually plotted the bank robberies. She had probably been the one who'd read Maggie's letters.

"This is perfect," the widow said with a smile of delight as she stood up with the gun clutched in her hands. At least the barrel was pointed at him instead of Maggie, who stood trembling on the other side of the coffee table from the deranged woman.

"This is stupid," Blaine corrected her. "There's nothing specifically linking you to the robberies. No evidence that you were aware of the crimes your husband and your brother were committing. You could have gotten away with it all."

Her smile vanished off her thin lips. "My brother?"

The woman obviously didn't care about herself right now—not when she planned to shoot two people with another federal agent posted right outside the door. But maybe she cared about her sibling.

"He was the one who tried abducting Maggie from Emergency," Blaine said. "He's a security guard at the hospital."

Tammy shook her head in denial. "The fact that he works there doesn't prove anything."

"His security badge will prove he was the one who opened the back door of the employees' locker room when he tried to kidnap Maggie." At least Blaine hoped it would. He needed evidence—not just suspicion—linking the man to the crimes.

"No…" But the conviction was gone from Tammy Doremire's voice as it began to quaver. "You can't tie him to the robberies…"

Maybe he wouldn't be able to, but he wasn't going to let her think that. "I have a team working on it right now. They're getting search warrants. They're digging into all of his financials. They're checking all his properties for any evidence linking him to the robberies. I'm pretty sure they'll find something. Aren't you?"

Her thin face tightened with dread and hatred. She knew that her brother wouldn't have gotten rid of all the evidence—or at least not the money. He could see she was torn, tempted to call and warn her brother about the warrants.

So he stepped closer, prepared to grab her weapon from her hands. Her eyes widened with alarm as she noticed that he'd closed some distance between them.

"Get back!" she yelled. "I'm going to kill her. You're not going to stop me this time."

"Why do you want her dead?" he asked. "If you hadn't sent your brother to the hospital after her, I wouldn't have linked him to the crimes." He was sure that her brother had acted on her orders; all the men probably had.

"It's all her fault!" Tammy yelled, as if she thought that saying it loud enough would make it true. "If she hadn't written those damn letters to Andy…"

A noise emanated from Maggie, but she'd muffled it with a hand over her mouth. She had already held herself responsible for the robberies; she didn't need this crazed woman compounding her guilt.

But making her feel guilty wasn't enough torment for Tammy Doremire. She intended to kill her, too.

"Who read them?" Blaine asked, stalling for time— hoping to distract the woman enough for Maggie to escape. He had left the apartment door open. Maybe Truman could get off a shot.

"I—I did," Tammy admitted.

As he'd suspected, she was the mastermind behind the robberies. He acted shocked, though, as he edged closer to her and that damn gun she gripped so tightly. "You read her personal correspondence to her fiancé?"

She snorted. "Personal? There hadn't been anything very personal about them. They were not *love* letters—not like I would have written to Mark—" her voice cracked with emotion, with loss "—if he'd been in a war zone."

She had loved her husband. The grief and pain contorted her face.

"Why didn't you take Mark to a hospital when he was hurt?" he asked. "Why did you drive him instead to that cabin in Michigan?"

"He—he wanted to go there," she said. "He knew he was dying—because of you. Because you shot him!" She pointed the gun at Blaine's chest.

And he was glad; it wasn't anywhere near Maggie

now. Maybe she could escape. Instead, she gasped in fear for him.

And her gasp drew Tammy's rage back to her. She whirled the gun in Maggie's direction. "But we wouldn't have been there if it wasn't for her. Mark just couldn't stay away from poor, sweet Maggie. She caused his death— just like she caused Andy's."

"That's bull." Blaine called her on her craziness. "I killed Mark—not Maggie. I pulled the trigger. Not Maggie."

She swung the gun back to him, and her eyes were wild with rage and grief. "It was your fault!"

"I shot him, but the vest should have protected him," Blaine said. "But he wasn't wearing *his* vest. He was wearing *yours*."

Tears began to streak down the woman's face as her own guilt overwhelmed her. She knew why her husband had died. But she couldn't accept her own part in his death. It was easier for her to blame him and Maggie.

She sniffled back her tears. And as she tried to clear her vision, he edged closer yet. "No…" she cried in protest of her guilt more than his nearness. "He shouldn't have died…"

He was counting on her not noticing how close he was to her. But she wasn't looking at him anymore; she had swung the gun back toward Maggie.

"Mark killed an innocent man," Maggie said in defense of Blaine shooting him. Of course she would defend him as she did everyone. "Why? Why would you two resort to stealing and killing?"

"Mark and I needed that money," Tammy said, desperately trying to justify their crimes. "We needed it to start our family."

"Hundreds of thousands of dollars?" Blaine scoffed.

He wanted to irritate her, wanted her to shoot at him instead of Maggie. He wore a vest. Maggie was completely unprotected.

"I—I couldn't get pregnant. I need—needed—fertility treatments. Or in vitro. All that's so expensive, and Mark lost his job." Now she wasn't just pointing the gun at Maggie but at her belly, and jealousy twisted the woman's face into a mask nearly as grotesque as the zombie one. "But this one—she easily gets pregnant."

Maggie held her hands over her belly, trying to protect her unborn baby. But her hands would prove no protection from a bullet.

"You don't want to hurt the baby," Blaine said, as horror gripped him. Maggie's baby was a part of her, and because he loved Maggie, he loved her baby, too. He couldn't lose either of them.

"She doesn't deserve that baby," Tammy said. "She never wanted it. She never wanted Andy. She didn't love him like I loved Mark. It's not fair."

"Life's not fair," Blaine commiserated.

But the woman didn't hear or see him anymore. It didn't matter that he was the one who'd fired the shot that had killed Mark. She hated Maggie more—she hated that the woman had what Tammy had wanted most. A baby…

And she intended to take that baby from Maggie before she took her life. He had to protect them. So Blaine did two things—he kicked the coffee table into the woman's legs and he grabbed for the gun.

But it went off. And a scream rang out. Maggie's scream.

Chapter Twenty-Two

Pain ripped through Maggie; she felt as if she were being torn in two. She patted her belly, but she felt no stickiness from blood, just an incredible tightness. She hadn't been shot. She'd gone into labor.

Blaine dropped to the ground beside her. "Where are you hit?"

She shook her head. "No…"

His hands replaced hers on her belly, and his green eyes widened. "You're in labor?"

"It's too soon," she said, as tears of pain and fear streamed down her face. "It's too soon. You have to stop it. I can't have the baby now."

Or Tammy Doremire would get her wish. Maggie wouldn't have the baby the woman didn't think she deserved. Maybe she was right.

Maggie probably didn't deserve her baby. But she wanted him. With all her heart she wanted him.

"We're going to get you to the hospital," Blaine said. "We're going to get you help." But his hand shook as he dialed 911, and his voice shook as he demanded an ambulance.

He was worried, too. Somehow Maggie found that reassuring, as if it proved he cared. If not about her, at least he cared about her baby. He showed he cared when he climbed into the ambulance with her and let Truman take Tammy Doremire into custody.

He took Maggie's hand, clasping it in both of his. "Everything's going to be okay," he promised. "Everything's going to be okay."

"Thank you," she managed between pants for breath. "Thank you."

His forehead furrowed and he asked, "For what?"

"You saved my life again," she said. And she hoped that he had saved the baby's, too.

But when they got to the hospital, it was too late. The doctors couldn't stop the labor. Her little boy was coming. "It's too early…"

"He'll be fine," Blaine assured her. "He's tough—like his mama."

Was she tough? Maggie had never felt as helpless and weak as she did at that moment. She couldn't stop her labor; she couldn't stop him from coming.

"Push," a nurse told her.

"I can't…" She shouldn't. But the urge was there—the urge to push him out. A contraction gripped her, tearing her apart again. There had been no time for them to administer an epidural. No time for them to ease her pain. She didn't care, though. She cared only about her baby. "It's too soon…"

"We'll take care of him," the doctor promised. "Push…"

Blaine touched her chin, tipping up her face so that she met his gaze. "You need to do this, Maggie. You've taken care of him as long as you could. Let the doctors take care of him now."

So she pushed, and her baby boy entered the world with a weak cry of protest.

"He's crying—that's good," Blaine assured her. "He's going to be okay."

But the doctors whisked him away, working on him. Were his lungs okay? Were they developed enough? Maggie had so many questions. But she didn't want to distract the doctors from her son, so she didn't ask any of them.

Blaine stroked his fingers along her cheek. "He'll be okay. He'll be okay. He's tough—just like you are."

Even though he'd repeated his assurance, Maggie couldn't accept it. She didn't feel tough. She felt shattered. Devastated. And Blaine must have seen that she was about to fall apart because he pulled her into his arms. And he held her. He held her together.

And not just then but over the next few days. He stayed with her at the hospital, making sure that she and the baby were all right. Maggie fell so far in love with him that she knew she would never get over him.

She didn't want to get over him. She wanted to be with him always. She wanted to be his wife—wanted her son to be his son, too.

The doctors already thought he was the little boy's father. They called him Dad, and Blaine never corrected them. But it wasn't his name on little Drew's birth certificate—it was Andy's as the father. He deserved that honor. He deserved to be with his son.

Andy was gone. Maggie had accepted that, but she wanted to honor him by giving his son his name. Blaine was with Maggie when the nurse brought in the baby from the neonatal unit. "He's breathing on his own, Mom," she said. "No more machines. He can stay in here with you."

"He's so tiny," Blaine said with wonder as he stared down at the sleeping infant.

"Drew's going to be a big boy," the nurse assured them. "He's doing very well for a preemie." She handed the baby to Maggie before leaving the room.

Her heart swelled with love as he automatically snuggled against her, as if he recognized her even though she hadn't carried him as long as she was supposed to.

"He's so tiny," Blaine repeated, still in awe.

"He's doing well, though," Maggie assured him.

"Drew?" Blaine asked.

Maybe she should have run the name past him first. But he had never indicated that he wanted a future with her and her son. So she hadn't wanted to presume.

She nodded.

"That's good. It's a good name," he said, his green gaze on the baby in her arms.

"I'm glad you think so," she said. She wanted him to be part of their lives. But even as she contemplated asking, he started pulling away.

He stood up. "Now that you're both okay, I need to get back to work on the case," he said. "I need to find the other robbers and make sure they don't try to go after you or Drew."

She shivered, and the baby awakened. But not with a cry. He opened his eyes just a little and stared calmly up at her. She had been in danger for too much of her pregnancy. She appreciated that Blaine wanted to make sure that they would finally be safe. But she wasn't sure that was really the reason he was leaving.

Or if he just wanted to get away from her. Maybe he didn't like that everyone had assumed he was the baby's father. Maybe he didn't want to be an instant daddy.

Before he left, he leaned over the bed, and he pressed a kiss to her lips and another to the baby's forehead. "I have a guard posted at the door. Truman will protect you. You'll be safe," he assured her.

"What about you?" she asked.

He grinned. "I'll be fine."

She couldn't help but remember that Andy had promised the same thing when he'd left for his last deployment. Would Blaine not return, as well?

BLAINE WOULDN'T PUT it past Tammy Doremire to set a trap for him. He interviewed her at the jail. In exchange for a lesser sentence, she gave him an address—not just for her brother but for the two coworkers who'd helped them pull off the robberies. He doubted she actually cared how much time she spent behind bars; she just wanted to make sure that Blaine was dead—like her husband.

"What did Maggie have?" she asked, as if she actually cared.

His blood chilled with a sense of foreboding. But he had guards posted at the hospital. They weren't hospital guards, either. Once he'd realized a hospital security guard had been involved in the robberies, he hadn't trusted any of them. Truman was inside Maggie's room, personally protecting her and Drew. He felt so bad about Tammy getting her alone that he would give up his life before he would let anyone hurt her or her baby again.

"A boy," he said.

"Of course," she said, as if she should have known. "Boys run in the Doremire family."

"She named him Drew," he said.

She shrugged, and her red hair brushed the shoulders of her orange jumpsuit. She looked nearly as bad as she had in the zombie mask. "Maybe she loved Andy more than I thought."

Maggie had loved her fiancé. He saw it in her face whenever she talked about him. She missed him.

Could Blaine fill the void Andy had left in her? He loved her so much that he wanted to try. But did he love her enough for both of them?

He had no idea how she actually felt about him. She had turned to him for protection—for comfort. But who else had she had now that Andy was gone?

Who else could she trust now that the family that had almost been hers had turned on her?

"That's too bad for you, huh?" Tammy remarked. "Since you love her…"

Blaine hadn't told Maggie his feelings; he wasn't about to tell this woman. He stood up and gestured toward a deputy to take Tammy back to holding. As they led her away, she turned back and smiled a sly smile.

She had definitely set a trap for him. So he was ready. He took Ash Stryker and Dalton Reyes with him as backup, along with some Michigan troopers. According to Tammy, her brother and his friends had gone back to the cabin. Supposedly she and Mark had stashed the money there. After finding the body, the dog tags and Maggie's letters, Blaine hadn't taken the time to search the entire area. Maybe the money was hidden there.

But Blaine suspected he wouldn't find just the money. Or the robbers.

"We could have called in more troopers," Ash remarked as he pulled his weapon from his holster.

But if Blaine had requested more, he might have had to use his sister, and he didn't want to put her in danger, too. He wanted her to be there to help Maggie and the baby in case he couldn't. He wanted Maggie to have a friend she could trust—unlike Susan Iverson or Tammy.

"You face down terrorists every day," Dalton Reyes teased him. "You're afraid of a few zombie bank robbers?"

"Some of the worst terrorists I've dealt with have been the homegrown kind, holed up in remote spots just like this one," Ash warned them. "They could have an arsenal in there."

Blaine sighed. "Oh, I'm sure that they do…"

He had no more than voiced the thought when gunfire erupted. It echoed throughout the woods, shattering the windows of the cabin and the windows of the vehicles he and the other agents had driven up.

He gestured at the others, indicating for them to go around the back as he headed straight toward the cabin. He was the one that they wanted—the one that Tammy Doremire wanted—dead.

Maggie had already lost one man who loved her. She shouldn't lose another—especially when Blaine had yet to tell her that he loved her. He should have told her…

He was afraid now that he might never have the chance. The gunfire continued. They had to have automatic weapons—maybe even armor-piercing bullets. The vest probably wouldn't help him—neither would the SWAT helmet he and the other agents wore.

Ignoring the risk, he returned fire. He had to take out these threats to Maggie and the baby. He had to make sure that they couldn't hurt her or Drew ever again. One man, wearing the zombie mask and trench-coat disguise, stepped out of the cabin. Blaine hit him, taking him down, but as the man fell, his automatic weapon continued to fire.

And Blaine felt the fiery sting as a bullet hit him. He ignored the pain as another robber exited the cabin, aiming straight for him. Even as his arm began to go numb, he kept squeezing the trigger. The zombie fell, but so did Blaine. He struck the ground hard.

His ears ringing from the gunshots, he could barely hear the others calling out for him. "Blaine! Blaine!"

"Are you hit?" Reyes asked.

"Where are you hit?" Ash asked.

He didn't even know—because what hurt the most

was his heart—at the thought that he might never see Maggie again. "Tell her…"

But he didn't have the strength to finish his request. Like Mark Doremire, he was afraid that he was about to bleed out in the woods.

All he managed to utter was her name. "Maggie…"

Chapter Twenty-Three

Maggie had suspected the worst even before Ash Stryker and another man walked into her hospital room. Their faces were pale with stress, and their clothes were smeared with blood that wasn't theirs. They looked unharmed but yet devastated.

"No…"

He couldn't be dead. Blaine couldn't have died without learning how much she loved him. How much she needed him…

He had always been there when she had needed him. Why hadn't she been there when he had needed her?

She was already out of bed, standing over Drew's clear bassinet. She stepped away from it, so that she wouldn't startle the sleeping baby. But her legs trembled, nearly giving way beneath her. Truman grabbed her, steadying her with a hand on her arm.

Ash shook his head. "He's not dead, Maggie," he said. "He's not dead."

"But he's hurt." They wouldn't look the way they did if he wasn't. "How badly?"

Ash shook his head again. "I don't know."

"Where was he shot?" she asked. "How many times?"

"What the hell happened?" Truman asked the question before she could add it to her others.

"We went back to that cabin," the other agent replied. "The woman told us the others were there getting the money she and her husband stashed somewhere on the property."

Maggie gasped. "Tammy wouldn't have helped Blaine. She wanted him dead."

"It was an ambush," the agent confirmed.

"But Blaine was expecting it," Ash said. "We got them all. It's over, Maggie."

But so might Blaine's life be over. "Where was he shot?" she asked again. "How many times?"

"Just once," the other agent replied. But from Mark's and Sarge's deaths, she knew once was enough to kill. "The bullet grazed the side of his neck."

"It nicked an artery," Ash said. "He lost a lot of blood."

"But he's alive," she said, clinging to hope.

Ash nodded but repeated, "He lost a lot of blood, though."

"The doctors aren't sure he's going to make it," the other man added. "After they stabilized him, they flew him here."

"Why?" There were hospitals closer to the cabin. Good ones.

"The last thing he said was your name," Ash told her.

So they'd thought he wanted to be with her? He had probably only been worried that Tammy had set a trap for her as well as him. She'd wanted them both dead.

But Maggie didn't care why they had brought Blaine here. She had to see him. She turned to Truman. "Can you keep an eye on Drew while I go see Blaine?"

"Of course," the big man replied, but he looked nervously at the tiny baby as if afraid that he might awaken.

"This way," Ash said, as he guided her down the hall

to an elevator. They took it to the ground floor and the intensive care unit.

"Only one person at a time," the nurse at the desk warned them.

Ash waved her forward, so she followed the nurse to Blaine's bedside. Her golden-haired superhero looked so vulnerable and pale lying there. An IV dripped fluids—maybe plasma—into him, probably replacing the blood he'd lost. A bandage covered the wound on his neck. The injury had been treated.

Now he just had to fight.

"Please," she implored him as she grasped his hand. "Please don't leave me." Tears overflowed her eyes, trailing down her face to drop onto his arm. "I can't lose you. You have to fight. You have to live."

Panic had her heart beating frantically, desperately. What could she do to help him fight? How could she lend him some of her strength, as he had always given her his? She wouldn't have survived without him. Even with all the robbers dead or in jail, she wasn't sure that she could survive now without him.

"Please," she implored him again, "please don't leave me."

His hand moved inside hers, his fingers entwining with hers. He squeezed. She glanced up at his face and found his green-eyed gaze focused on her. He was conscious!

Embarrassed that he'd caught her crying all over him, she felt heat flood her face. "I'm sorry," she said.

"Sorry?" he asked, his voice a husky rasp.

"I—I'm crying all over you," she pointed out. "And I'm making assumptions."

"Assumptions?"

"I shouldn't have assumed that you're with me," she

said. "I know that you've just been protecting me—that you've just been doing your job—"

He tugged his hand from hers and pressed his fingers over her lips. "Shh…"

The man was exhausted, and here she was, rambling away. She had always talked too much.

"I'm sorry," she murmured again—against his fingers.

He shook his head—weakly. "You're wrong…"

Before he could tell her what she was wrong about, the nurse stepped back into the area. "He's awake? Mr. Campbell, you're conscious!" She leaned over and flashed a light in his eyes.

Blaine squinted and cursed. "Yes, I'm conscious."

"I have to get the doctor!" the nurse exclaimed as she hurried off.

"I should go," Maggie said. "I should tell Ash that you're awake." His friends had been worried about him, too.

"I think he probably heard," Blaine pointed out, as the nurse's voice rang out.

"Then he'll want to see you," Maggie said. She tugged on her hand, trying to free it from his so that she could escape before she suffered even more embarrassment. But before she could leave, a doctor hurried over with the excited nurse.

But even while the doctor talked to him—telling Blaine how lucky he was—he wouldn't release her. While she loved the warmth and comfort of his hand holding hers, she dreaded the moment when they would be alone again. Because even though he hadn't died, she suspected he would still be leaving her.

BLAINE WAS GRATEFUL to the doctor for saving his life, but he couldn't wait to get rid of him and the nurse. He wanted to be alone with Maggie again.

But the doctor wouldn't stop talking. "You're going to need to take it easy for a while and let your body recover from the blood loss. We're going to keep you in ICU overnight. You really need your rest."

"I should leave," Maggie said again as she tried to tug her hand free of his.

He wouldn't let her go, though. He was strong enough to hang on to her. She gave him strength. Hearing her sweet voice had drawn him from the fog of unconsciousness. She'd made him want to fight. Had made him want to live...

For her.

With her.

"No," he said. "I need to talk to you." And he gave a pointed look to the doctor and nurse, who finally took his not-so-subtle hint and left them alone.

"It's okay," she said. "I understand. You don't have to explain to me that you were just doing your job—protecting me and Drew. I know that you don't feel the same way about me that I do about you."

He reached out again and covered her silky soft lips with his fingers. "Sweetheart, you do talk too much." She'd said it herself, but until now he hadn't agreed with her.

"Sweetheart?" She mouthed the word against his fingers.

"But that's the only thing you're right about," he said. "You're wrong about everything else."

She stopped trying to talk now, and she waited for him to speak. That had never been easy for him—to share his feelings. He'd been hiding them for too long.

And obviously he'd hidden them too well from Maggie because she had no idea how he felt about her.

"You were never just a job to me," he said. "If you

were, I wouldn't have had to protect you myself. I would have trusted you to Truman or someone like him way before I had to—"

"But you did," she murmured against his fingers.

"I had to," he said, "or I was never going to figure out who was trying to hurt you and the baby. But it killed me to not be with you every day." And when he'd had to leave them again—after Drew had been born—it had literally nearly killed him. "I don't want to be away from you and Drew again."

Tears began to shimmer in those enormous brown eyes of hers. "Blaine…?"

He knew what he wanted to say, but he didn't know how to say it. "I don't have a ring…"

He couldn't forget the size and shine of the diamond Andy had given her. But Andy was gone. She had accepted that; Blaine needed to accept it, too.

"And I can't get down on one knee right now…" Hanging on to her hand had sapped all his strength. If he tried getting out of bed, he would undoubtedly pass out at her feet.

"I don't need a ring," she said. "I don't need any gestures. I just need to know how you feel about me."

"I'm not good at expressing my feelings," he said apologetically.

"Just tell me…"

"I love you," he said. "I love your sweetness and your openness. I love how you worry and care about everyone and everything."

"You love me?"

He nodded. "I know I'm not your first choice and that you'd promised to marry another man. But Andy's gone. And I'm here. And I will love you as much as he would have—if not more. I will take care of you and Drew. I will treat your son just like he's mine, too, if you'll let me."

The tears overflowed her eyes and spilled down her cheeks. "I don't deserve you," she said. "And I didn't deserve Andy. Tammy was right about that. I didn't love him like I should have. I loved him because he was my best friend. I didn't love him like a woman should love the man she wants to marry. And I didn't want to marry him. But I didn't know how to say no to his proposal without hurting him."

And with her big, loving heart, she would have given up her own happiness to ensure someone else's. He didn't want her doing that for him.

"You won't hurt me if you tell me no," he lied. It would hurt him. But he'd heard what she'd said when she'd thought him unconscious. He didn't think she would tell him no. But he wanted her to say yes for the right reasons. "You'll hurt me if you say yes and don't really love me."

"I love you," she said. "I love you like a woman loves a man. I love you with passion. I love you like a soul mate, not just as a friend."

The tightness in his chest eased, and he grinned. "I love how much you talk," he said. "I really do...especially when you're telling me how much you love me." But then he realized what she had yet to say. "But you haven't answered my question."

"Did you ask me something?" she asked with a coy flutter of her lashes.

"I will get out of this bed," he said, but they both knew it was an empty threat at the moment.

"I don't need the bended knee or the ring," she said. "I just need the question."

So he asked, "Will you marry me, Maggie Jenkins? Will you take me as your husband and as Drew's father?"

"Yes, Special Agent Blaine Campbell," she replied. "I will marry you."

He used their joined hands to tug her closer, to pull her down for the kiss to seal their promise.

Someone cleared his throat above the sound of a baby crying. "Excuse me," Truman said. "But someone was looking for his mama…" The burly agent carried the tiny fussing baby over to Maggie.

She laid the little boy on Blaine's chest, and the baby's cries stopped. He stared up at Blaine as if he recognized him. "Here's your daddy," she said.

Blaine had a perfect record—every case solved with the FBI, every criminal caught—but this—his family—meant far more to him. This woman and their child was what made his life special now and for always.

* * * * *

REQUEST YOUR FREE BOOKS!
2 FREE NOVELS PLUS 2 FREE GIFTS!

HARLEQUIN®

INTRIGUE®

BREATHTAKING ROMANTIC SUSPENSE

YES! Please send me 2 FREE Harlequin Intrigue® novels and my 2 FREE gifts (gifts are worth about $10). After receiving them, if I don't wish to receive any more books, I can return the shipping statement marked "cancel." If I don't cancel, I will receive 6 brand-new novels every month and be billed just $4.74 per book in the U.S. or $5.24 per book in Canada. That's a savings of at least 14% off the cover price! It's quite a bargain! Shipping and handling is just 50¢ per book in the U.S. and 75¢ per book in Canada.* I understand that accepting the 2 free books and gifts places me under no obligation to buy anything. I can always return a shipment and cancel at any time. Even if I never buy another book, the two free books and gifts are mine to keep forever.

182/382 HDN F42N

Name	(PLEASE PRINT)

Address	Apt. #

City	State/Prov.	Zip/Postal Code

Signature (if under 18, a parent or guardian must sign)

Mail to the **Harlequin® Reader Service:**
IN U.S.A.: P.O. Box 1867, Buffalo, NY 14240-1867
IN CANADA: P.O. Box 609, Fort Erie, Ontario L2A 5X3
**Are you a subscriber to Harlequin Intrigue books
and want to receive the larger-print edition?
Call 1-800-873-8635 or visit www.ReaderService.com.**

* Terms and prices subject to change without notice. Prices do not include applicable taxes. Sales tax applicable in N.Y. Canadian residents will be charged applicable taxes. Offer not valid in Quebec. This offer is limited to one order per household. Not valid for current subscribers to Harlequin Intrigue books. All orders subject to credit approval. Credit or debit balances in a customer's account(s) may be offset by any other outstanding balance owed by or to the customer. Please allow 4 to 6 weeks for delivery. Offer available while quantities last.

Your Privacy—The Harlequin® Reader Service is committed to protecting your privacy. Our Privacy Policy is available online at www.ReaderService.com or upon request from the Harlequin Reader Service.

We make a portion of our mailing list available to reputable third parties that offer products we believe may interest you. If you prefer that we not exchange your name with third parties, or if you wish to clarify or modify your communication preferences, please visit us at www.ReaderService.com/consumerschoice or write to us at Harlequin Reader Service Preference Service, P.O. Box 9062, Buffalo, NY 14269. Include your complete name and address.

HI13R

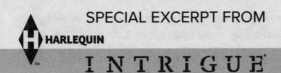
Nick Darcy woke to the sort of darkness that one found
miles from a big city. No ambient light tempered the deep
gloom, and the only noise was the sound of his heart
pounding a rapid cadence of panic against his breastbone.

Just a dream.

Except it hadn't been. The embassy siege had happened. People had died, some in the most brutal ways
imaginable.

And he'd been unable to save them.

He pushed the stem of his watch, lighting up the dial.
Four in the morning. Sitting up on the edge of the sofa,
he started to reach for the switch of the lamp on the table
beside him when he heard a soft thump come from
outside the cabin. His nerves, still in fight-or-flight mode,
vibrated like the taut strings of a violin.

Leaving the light off, he reached for his SIG Sauer
P229 and eased it from the pancake holster lying on the
coffee table in front of the sofa.

The noises could be coming from a scavenging raccoon venturing onto the cabin porch or the wind knocking a dead limb from one of the blight-ridden Fraser firs surrounding his cabin.

But between his years with the DSS and the past few months he'd been working for Alexander Quinn at The Gates, he knew that bumps in the night could also mean deadly trouble.

As he moved silently toward the front door, he heard another sound from outside. A soft thump against the door, half knock, half scrape.

There was no security lens set into the heavy wood front door of the cabin, a failing he made a mental note to rectify as soon as possible. He improvised, edging toward the window that looked out onto the porch and angling his gaze toward the welcome mat in front of the door.

The view was obstructed by the angle, but he thought he could make out a dark mass lying on the porch floor in front of the door.

He checked the gun's magazine and chambered a round before he pulled open the front door.

A woman spilled inside and crumpled at his feet.

Don't miss
KILLSHADOW ROAD by Paula Graves,
available in April 2015 wherever
Harlequin Intrigue® books and ebooks are sold.

www.Harlequin.com

JUST CAN'T GET ENOUGH
ROMANCE
Looking for more?

5425

Harlequin has everything from contemporary, passionate and heartwarming to suspenseful and inspirational stories.

Whatever your mood,
we have a romance just for you!

Connect with us to find your next great read,
special offers and more.

Facebook.com/HarlequinBooks
Twitter.com/HarlequinBooks
HarlequinBlog.com
Harlequin.com/Newsletters

H HARLEQUIN®

A *Romance* FOR EVERY MOOD™

www.Harlequin.com